THE MOORLAND COTTAGE

Elizabeth Cleghorn Gaskell 1810-1865

Cover Painting:

"A Cottage Garden" by Curtius Duassut (1889-1903).

Cover Design Copyright © 2007 by Vera Nazarian

ISBN-13: 978-1-934648-29-2
ISBN-10: 1-934648-29-9

First Publication: 1850.

Reprint Trade Paperback Edition

November 2007

A Publication of
Norilana Books
P. O. Box 2188
Winnetka, CA 91396
www.norilana.com

Printed in the United States of America

The Moorland Cottage

Norilana Books
Classics

www.norilana.com

The

Moorland

Cottage

❧⟨❦⟩❧

Elizabeth

Gaskell

❧⟨❦⟩❧

Chapter I.

If you take the turn to the left, after you pass the lyke-gate at Combehurst Church, you will come to the wooden bridge over the brook; keep along the field-path which mounts higher and higher, and, in half a mile or so, you will be in a breezy upland field, almost large enough to be called a down, where sheep pasture on the short, fine, elastic turf. You look down on Combehurst and its beautiful church-spire. After the field is crossed, you come to a common, richly colored with the golden gorse and the purple heather, which in summer-time send out their warm scents into the quiet air. The swelling waves of the upland make a near horizon against the sky; the line is only broken in one place by a small grove of Scotch firs, which always look black and shadowed even at mid-day, when all the rest of the landscape seems bathed in sunlight. The lark quivers and sings high up in the air; too high—in too dazzling a region for you to see her. Look! she drops into sight; but, as if loath to leave the heavenly radiance, she balances herself and floats in the ether. Now she falls suddenly right into her nest, hidden among the ling, unseen except by the eyes of Heaven, and the small bright insects that run hither and thither on the elastic flower-stalks. With something like the sudden drop of the lark, the path goes down a green abrupt descent; and in a basin, surrounded by the grassy hills, there stands a dwelling, which is neither cottage nor house, but something between the two in size. Nor yet is it a farm, though surrounded by living things. It is, or rather it was, at the time of which I speak, the dwelling of Mrs. Browne, the widow of the late curate of Combehurst. There she lived with her faithful old servant and her only children, a boy and girl. They were as secluded in their green hollow as the households in the German forest-tales. Once a week they emerged and crossed the common, catching on its summit the first sounds of the sweet-toned bells, calling them to church. Mrs. Browne walked first, holding Edward's hand. Old Nancy followed with Maggie; but they were all one party, and all talked together in a subdued and quiet tone, as beseemed the day. They had not much to say, their lives were too unbroken; for, excepting on Sundays, the widow and her children never went to Combehurst. Most people would have thought the little town a quiet, dreamy place; but to those two children it seemed the world; and after they had crossed the bridge, they each clasped more tightly the hands which they held, and looked shyly up from beneath their drooped eyelids when spoken to by any of their mother's friends. Mrs. Browne was regularly asked by some one to stay to dinner after morning church, and as regularly declined, rather to the timid children's relief; although in the week-days they sometimes spoke together in a low voice of the pleasure it would be to them if mamma would go and dine at Mr. Buxton's, where the little girl in white and that great tall boy lived. Instead of staying there, or anywhere else, on Sundays, Mrs. Browne thought it her duty to go and cry over her husband's grave. The custom had arisen out of true sorrow for his loss, for a kinder husband, and more worthy man, had never lived; but the simplicity of her sorrow had been destroyed by the observation of others on the mode of its manifestation. They made way for her to cross the grass toward his grave; and she, fancying that it was expected of her, fell into the habit I have mentioned. Her children, holding each a hand, felt awed and uncomfortable, and were sensitively conscious how often they were pointed out, as a mourning group, to observation.

"I wish it would always rain on Sundays," said Edward one day to Maggie, in a garden conference.

"Why?" asked she.

"Because then we bustle out of church, and get home as fast as we can, to save mamma's crape; and we have not to go and cry over papa."

"I don't cry," said Maggie. "Do you?"

Edward looked round before he answered, to see if they were quite alone, and then said:

"No; I was sorry a long time about papa, but one can't go on being sorry forever. Perhaps grown-up people can."

"Mamma can," said little Maggie. "Sometimes I am very sorry too; when I am by myself or playing with you, or when I am wakened up by the moonlight in our room. Do you ever waken and fancy you heard papa calling you? I do sometimes; and then I am very sorry to think we shall never hear him calling us again."

"Ah, it's different with me, you know. He used to call me to lessons."

"Sometimes he called me when he was displeased with me. But I always dream that he was calling us in his own kind voice, as he used to do when he wanted us to walk with him, or to show us something pretty."

Edward was silent, playing with something on the ground. At last he looked round again, and, having convinced himself that they could not be overheard, he whispered:

"Maggie—sometimes I don't think I'm sorry that papa is dead—when I'm naughty, you know; he would have been so angry with me if he had been here; and I think—only sometimes, you know, I'm rather glad he is not."

"Oh, Edward! you don't mean to say so, I know. Don't let us talk about him. We can't talk rightly, we're such little children. Don't, Edward, please."

Poor little Maggie's eyes filled with tears; and she never spoke again to Edward, or indeed to any one, about her dead father. As she grew older, her life became more actively busy. The cottage and small outbuildings, and the garden and field, were their own; and on the produce they depended for much of their support. The cow, the pig, and the poultry took up much of Nancy's time. Mrs. Browne and Maggie had to do a great deal of the house-work; and when the beds were made, and the rooms swept and dusted, and the preparations for dinner ready, then, if there was any time, Maggie sat down to her lessons. Ned, who prided himself considerably on his sex, had been sitting all the morning, in his father's arm-chair, in the little book-room, "studying," as he chose to call it. Sometimes Maggie would pop her head in, with a request that he would help her to carry the great pitcher of water up-stairs, or do some other little household service; with which request he occasionally complied, but with so many complaints about the interruption, that at last she told him she would never ask him again. Gently as this was said, he yet felt it as a reproach, and tried to excuse himself.

"You see, Maggie, a man must be educated to be a gentleman. Now, if a woman knows how to keep a house, that's all that is wanted from her. So my time is of more consequence than yours. Mamma says I'm to go to college, and be a clergyman; so I must get on with my Latin."

Maggie submitted in silence; and almost felt it as an act of gracious condescension when, a morning or two afterwards, he came to meet her as she was toiling in from the well, carrying the great brown jug full of spring-water ready for dinner. "Here," said he, "let us put it in the shade behind the horse-mount. Oh, Maggie! look what you've done! Spilt it all, with not turning quickly enough when I told you. Now you may fetch it again for yourself, for I'll have nothing to do with it."

"I did not understand you in time," said she, softly. But he had turned away, and gone back in offended dignity to the house. Maggie had nothing to do but return to the well, and fill it again. The spring was some distance off, in a little rocky dell. It was so cool after her hot walk, that she sat down in the shadow of the gray limestone rock, and looked at the ferns, wet with the dripping water. She felt sad, she knew not why. "I think Ned is sometimes very cross," thought she. "I did not understand he was carrying it there. Perhaps I am clumsy. Mamma says I am; and Ned says I am. Nancy never says so and papa never said so. I wish I could help being clumsy and stupid. Ned says all women are so. I wish I was not a woman. It must be a fine thing to be a man. Oh dear! I must go up the field again with this heavy pitcher, and my arms do so ache!" She rose and climbed the steep brae. As she went she heard her mother's voice.

"Maggie! Maggie! there's no water for dinner, and the potatoes are quite boiled. Where *is* that child?"

They had begun dinner, before she came down from brushing her hair and washing her hands. She was hurried and tired.

"Mother," said Ned, "mayn't I have some butter to these potatoes, as there is cold meat? They are so dry."

"Certainly, my dear. Maggie, go and fetch a pat of butter out of the dairy."

Maggie went from her untouched dinner without speaking.

"Here, stop, you child!" said Nancy, turning her back in the passage. "You go to your dinner, I'll fetch the butter. You've been running about enough to-day."

Maggie durst not go back without it, but she stood in the passage till Nancy returned; and then she put up her mouth to be kissed by the kind rough old servant.

"Thou'rt a sweet one," said Nancy to herself, as she turned into the kitchen; and Maggie went back to her dinner with a soothed and lightened heart.

When the meal was ended, she helped her mother to wash up the old-fashioned glasses and spoons, which were treated with tender care and exquisite cleanliness in that house of decent frugality; and then, exchanging her pinafore for a black silk apron, the little maiden was wont to sit down to some useful piece of needlework, in doing which her mother enforced the most dainty neatness of stitches. Thus every hour in its circle brought a duty to be fulfilled; but duties fulfilled are as pleasures to the memory, and little Maggie always thought those early childish days most happy, and remembered them only as filled with careless contentment.

Yet, at the time they had their cares.

In fine summer days Maggie sat out of doors at her work. Just beyond the court lay the rocky moorland, almost as gay as that with its profusion of flowers. If the court had its clustering noisettes, and fraxinellas, and sweetbriar, and great tall white lilies, the moorland had its little creeping scented rose, its straggling honeysuckle, and an abundance of yellow cistus; and here and there a gray rock cropped out of the ground, and over it the yellow stone-crop and scarlet-leaved crane's-bill grew luxuriantly. Such a rock was Maggie's seat. I believe she considered it her own, and loved it accordingly; although its real owner was a great lord, who lived far away, and had never seen the moor, much less the piece of gray rock, in his life.

The afternoon of the day which I have begun to tell you about, she was sitting there, and singing to herself as she worked: she was within call of home, and could hear all home sounds, with their shrillness softened down. Between her and it, Edward was amusing himself; he often called upon her for sympathy, which she as readily gave.

"I wonder how men make their boats steady; I have taken mine to the pond, and she has toppled over every time I sent her in."

"Has it?—that's very tiresome! Would if do to put a little weight in it, to keep it down?"

"How often must I tell you to call a ship 'her;' and there you will go on saying—it—it!"

After this correction of his sister, Master Edward did not like the condescension of acknowledging her suggestion to be a good one; so he went silently to the house in search of the requisite ballast; but not being able to find anything suitable, he came back to his turfy hillock, littered round with chips of wood, and tried to insert some pebbles into his vessel; but they stuck fast, and he was obliged to ask again.

"Supposing it was a good thing to weight her, what could I put in?"

Maggie thought a moment.

"Would shot do?" asked she.

"It would be the very thing; but where can I get any?"

"There is some that was left of papa's. It is in the right-hand corner of the second drawer of the bureau, wrapped up in a newspaper."

"What a plague! I can't remember your 'seconds,' and 'right-hands,' and fiddle-faddles." He worked on at his pebbles. They would hot do.

"I think if you were good-natured, Maggie, you might go for me."

"Oh, Ned! I've all this long seam to do. Mamma said I must finish it before tea; and that I might play a little if I had done if first," said Maggie, rather plaintively; for it was a real pain to her to refuse a request.

"It would not take you five minutes."

Maggie thought a little. The time would only be taken out of her playing, which, after all, did not signify; while Edward was really busy about his ship. She rose, and clambered up the steep grassy slope, slippery with the heat.

Before she had found the paper of shot, she heard her mother's voice calling, in a sort of hushed hurried loudness, as if anxious to be heard by one person yet not by another—"Edward, Edward, come home quickly. Here's Mr. Buxton coming along the Fell-Lane;—he's coming here, as sure as sixpence; come, Edward, come."

Maggie saw Edward put down his ship and come. At his mother's bidding it certainly was; but he strove to make this as little apparent as he could, by sauntering up the slope, with his hands in his pockets, in a very independent and *négligé* style. Maggie had no time to watch longer; for now she was called too, and down stairs she ran.

"Here, Maggie," said her mother, in a nervous hurry;— "help Nancy to get a tray ready all in a minute. I do believe here's Mr. Buxton coming to call. Oh, Edward! go and brush your hair, and put on your Sunday jacket; here's Mr. Buxton just coming round. I'll only run up and change my cap; and you say you'll come up and tell me, Nancy; all proper, you know."

"To be sure, ma'am. I've lived in families afore now," said Nancy, gruffly.

"Oh, yes, I know you have. Be sure you bring in the cowslip wine. I wish I could have stayed to decant some port."

Nancy and Maggie bustled about, in and out of the kitchen and dairy; and were so deep in their preparations for Mr. Buxton's reception that they were not aware of the very presence of that gentleman himself on the scene. He had found the front door open, as is the wont in country places, and had walked in; first stopping at the empty parlor, and then finding his way to the place where voices and sounds proclaimed that there were inhabitants. So he stood there, stooping a little under the low-browed lintels of the kitchen door, and looking large, and red, and warm, but with a pleased and almost amused expression of face.

"Lord bless me, sir! what a start you gave me!" said Nancy, as she suddenly caught sight of him. "I'll go and tell my missus in a minute that you're come."

Off she went, leaving Maggie alone with the great, tall, broad gentleman, smiling at her from his frame in the door-way, but never speaking. She went on dusting a wine-glass most assiduously.

"Well done, little girl," came out a fine strong voice at last. "Now I think that will do. Come and show me the parlor where I may sit down, for I've had a long walk, and am very tired."

Maggie took him into the parlor, which was always cool and fresh in the hottest weather. It was scented by a great beau-pot filled with roses; and, besides, the casement was open to the fragrant court. Mr. Buxton was so large, and the parlor so small, that when he was once in, Maggie thought when he went away, he could carry the room on his back, as a snail does its house.

"And so, you are a notable little woman, are you?" said he, after he had stretched himself (a very unnecessary proceeding), and unbuttoned his waistcoat, Maggie stood near the door, uncertain whether to go or to stay. "How bright and clean you were making that glass! Do you think you could get me some water to fill it? Mind, it must be that very glass I saw you polishing. I shall know it again."

Maggie was thankful to escape out of the room; and in the passage she met her mother, who had made time to change her gown as well as her cap. Before Nancy would allow the little girl to return with the glass of water she smoothed her short-cut glossy hair; it was all that was needed to make her look delicately neat. Maggie was conscientious in trying to find out the identical glass; but I am afraid Nancy was not quite so truthful in avouching that one of the six, exactly similar, which were now placed on the tray, was the same she had found on the dresser, when she came back from telling her mistress of Mr. Buxton's arrival.

Maggie carried in the water, with a shy pride in the clearness of the glass. Her mother was sitting on the edge of her chair, speaking in unusually fine language, and with a higher pitched voice than common. Edward, in all his Sunday glory, was standing by Mr. Buxton, looking happy and conscious. But when Maggie came in, Mr. Buxton made room for her between Edward and himself, and, while she went on talking, lifted her on to his knee. She sat there as on a pinnacle of honor; but as she durst not nestle up to him, a chair would have been the more comfortable seat.

"As founder's line, I have a right of presentation; and for my dear old friend's sake" (here Mrs. Browne wiped her eyes), "I am truly glad of it; my young friend will have a little form of examination to go through; and then we shall see him carrying every prize before him, I have no doubt. Thank you, just a little of your sparkling cowslip wine. Ah! this gingerbread is like the gingerbread I had when I was a boy. My little lady here must learn the receipt, and make me some. Will she?"

"Speak to Mr. Buxton, child, who is kind to your brother. You will make him some gingerbread, I am sure."

"If I may," said Maggie, hanging down her head.

"Or, I'll tell you what. Suppose you come to my house, and teach us how to make it there; and then, you know, we could always be making gingerbread when we were not eating it. That would be best, I think. Must I ask mamma to bring you down to Combehurst, and let us all get acquainted together? I have a great boy and a little girl at home, who will like to see you, I'm sure. And we have got a pony for you to ride on, and a peacock and guinea fowls, and I don't know what all. Come, madam, let me persuade you. School begins in three weeks. Let us fix a day before then."

"Do mamma," said Edward.

"I am not in spirits for visiting," Mrs. Browne answered. But the quick children detected a hesitation in her manner of saying the oft spoken words, and had hopes, if only Mr. Buxton would persevere in his invitation.

"Your not visiting is the very reason why you are not in spirits. A little change, and a few neighborly faces, would do you good, I'll be bound. Besides, for the children's sake you should not live too secluded a life. Young people should see a little of the world."

Mrs. Browne was much obliged to Mr. Buxton for giving her so decent an excuse for following her inclination, which, it must be owned, tended to the acceptance of the invitation. So, "for the children's sake," she consented. But she sighed, as if making a sacrifice.

"That's right," said Mr. Buxton. "Now for the day."

It was fixed that they should go on that day week; and after some further conversation about the school at which Edward was to be placed, and some more jokes about Maggie's notability, and an inquiry if she would come and live with him the next time he wanted a housemaid, Mr. Buxton took his leave.

His visit had been an event; and they made no great attempt at settling again that day to any of their usual employments. In the first place, Nancy came in to hear and discuss all the proposed plans. Ned, who was uncertain whether to like or dislike the prospect of school, was very much offended by the old servant's remark, on first hearing of the project.

"It's time for him. He'll learn his place there, which, it strikes me, he and others too are apt to forget at home."

Then followed discussions and arrangements respecting his clothes. And then they came to the plan of spending a day at Mr. Buxton's, which Mrs. Browne was rather shy of mentioning, having a sort of an idea of inconstancy and guilt connected with the thought of mingling with the world again. However, Nancy approved: "It was quite right," and "just as it should be," and "good for the children."

"Yes; it was on their account I did it, Nancy," said Mrs. Browne.

"How many children has Mr. Buxton?" asked Edward.

"Only one. Frank, I think, they call him. But you must say Master Buxton; be sure."

"Who is the little girl, then," asked Maggie, "who sits with them in church?"

"Oh! that's little Miss Harvey, his niece, and a great fortune."

"They do say he never forgave her mother till the day of her death," remarked Nancy.

"Then they tell stories, Nancy!" replied Mrs. Browne (it was she herself who had said it; but that was before Mr. Buxton's call). For d'ye think his sister would have left him guardian to her child, if they were not on good terms?"

"Well! I only know what folks say. And, for sure, he took a spite at Mr. Harvey for no reason on earth; and every one knows he never spoke to him."

"He speaks very kindly and pleasantly," put in Maggie.

"Ay; and I'm not saying but what he is a very good, kind man in the main. But he has his whims, and keeps hold on 'em when he's got 'em. There's them pies burning, and I'm talking here!"

When Nancy had returned to her kitchen, Mrs. Browne called Maggie up stairs, to examine what clothes would be needed for Edward. And when they were up, she tried on the black satin gown, which had been her visiting dress ever since she was married, and which she intended should replace the old, worn-out bombazine on the day of the visit to Combehurst.

"For Mrs. Buxton is a real born lady," said she; "and I should like to be well dressed, to do her honor."

"I did not know there was a Mrs. Buxton," said Maggie. "She is never at church."

"No; she is but delicate and weakly, and never leaves the house. I think her maid told me she never left her room now."

The Buxton family, root and branch, formed the *pièce de résistance* in the conversation between Mrs. Browne and her children for the next week. As the day drew near, Maggie almost wished to stay at home, so impressed was she with the awfulness of the visit. Edward felt bold in the idea of a new suit of clothes, which had been ordered for the occasion, and for school afterwards. Mrs. Browne remembered having heard the rector say, "A woman never looked so lady-like as when she wore black satin," and kept her spirits up with that observation; but when she saw how worn it was at the elbows, she felt rather depressed, and unequal to visiting. Still, for her children's sake, she would do much.

After her long day's work was ended, Nancy sat up at her sewing. She had found out that among all the preparations, none were going on for Margaret; and she had used her influence over her mistress (who half-liked and half-feared, and entirely depended upon her) to obtain from her an old gown, which she had taken to pieces, and washed and scoured, and was now making up, in a way a little old-fashioned to be sure; but, on the whole, it looked so nice when completed and put on, that Mrs. Browne gave Maggie a strict lecture about taking great care of such a handsome frock and forgot that she had considered the gown from which if had been made as worn out and done for.

Chapter II.

At length they were dressed, and Nancy stood on the court-steps, shading her eyes, and looking after them, as they climbed the heathery slope leading to Combehurst.

"I wish she'd take her hand sometimes, just to let her know the feel of her mother's hand. Perhaps she will, at least after Master Edward goes to school."

As they went along, Mrs. Browne gave the children a few rules respecting manners and etiquette.

"Maggie! you must sit as upright as ever you can; make your back flat, child, and don't poke. If I cough, you must draw up. I shall cough whenever I see you do anything wrong, and I shall be looking at you all day; so remember. You hold yourself very well, Edward. If Mr. Buxton asks you, you may have a glass of wine, because you're a boy. But mind and say, 'Your good health, sir,' before you drink it."

"I'd rather not have the wine if I'm to say that," said Edward, bluntly.

"Oh, nonsense! my dear. You'd wish to be like a gentleman, I'm sure."

Edward muttered something which was inaudible. His mother went on:

Of course you'll never think of being helped more than twice. Twice of meat, twice of pudding, is the genteel thing. You may take less, but never more."

"Oh, mamma! how beautiful Combehurst spire is, with that dark cloud behind it!" exclaimed Maggie, as they came in sight of the town.

"You've no business with Combehurst spire when I'm speaking to you. I'm talking myself out of breath to teach you how to behave, and there you go looking after clouds, and such like rubbish. I'm ashamed of you."

Although Maggie walked quietly by her mother's side all the rest of the way, Mrs. Browne was too much offended to resume her instructions on good-breeding. Maggie might be helped three times if she liked: she had done with her.

They were very early. When they drew near the bridge, they were met by a tall, fine-looking boy, leading a beautiful little Shetland pony, with a side-saddle on it. He came up to Mrs. Browne, and addressed her.

"My father thought your little girl would be tired, and he told me to bring my cousin Erminia's pony for her. It's as quiet as can be."

Now this was rather provoking to Mrs. Browne, as she chose to consider Maggie in disgrace. However, there was no help for it: all she could do was to spoil the enjoyment as far as possible, by looking and speaking in a cold manner, which often chilled Maggie's little heart, and took all the zest out of the pleasure now. It was in vain that Frank Buxton made the pony trot and canter; she still looked sad and grave.

"Little dull thing!" he thought; but he was as kind and considerate as a gentlemanly boy could be.

At last they reached Mr. Buxton's house. It was in the main street, and the front door opened upon it by a flight of steps. Wide on each side extended the stone-coped windows. It was in reality a mansion, and needed not the neighboring contrast of the cottages on either side to make it look imposing. When they went in, they entered a large hall, cool even on that burning July day, with a black and white flag floor, and old settees round the walls, and great jars of curious china, which were filled with pot-pourrie. The dusky gloom was pleasant, after the glare of the street outside; and the requisite light and cheerfulness were given by the peep into the garden, framed, as it were, by the large door-way that opened into it. There were roses, and sweet-peas, and poppies—a rich mass of color, which looked well, set in the somewhat sombre coolness of the hall. All the house told of wealth—wealth which had accumulated for generations, and which was shown in a sort of comfortable, grand, unostentatious way. Mr. Buxton's ancestors had been yeomen; but, two or three generations back, they might, if ambitious, have taken their place as country gentry, so much had the value of their property increased, and so great had been the amount of their savings. They, however, continued to live in the old farm till Mr. Buxton's grandfather built the house in Combehurst of which I am speaking, and then he felt rather ashamed of what he had done; it seemed like stepping out of his position. He and his wife always sat in the best kitchen; and it was only after his son's marriage that the entertaining rooms were furnished. Even then they were kept with closed shutters and bagged-up furniture during the lifetime of the old couple, who, nevertheless, took a pride in adding to the rich-fashioned ornaments and grand old china of the apartments. But they died, and were gathered to their fathers, and young Mr. and Mrs. Buxton (aged respectively fifty-one and forty-five) reigned in their stead. They had the good taste to make no sudden change; but gradually the rooms assumed an inhabited appearance, and their son and daughter grew up in the enjoyment of great wealth, and no small degree of refinement. But as yet they held back modestly from putting themselves in any way on a level with the county people. Lawrence Buxton was sent to the same school as his father had been before him; and the notion of his going to college to complete his education was, after some deliberation, negatived. In process of time he succeeded his father, and married a sweet, gentle lady, of a decayed and very poor county family, by whom he had one boy before she fell into delicate health. His sister had married a man whose character was worse than his fortune, and had been left a widow. Everybody thought her husband's death a blessing; but she loved him, in spite of negligence and many grosser faults; and so, not many years after, she died, leaving her little daughter to her brother's care, with many a broken-voiced entreaty that he would never speak a word against the dead father of her child. So the little Erminia was taken home by her self-reproaching uncle, who felt now how hardly he had acted towards his sister in breaking off all communication with her on her ill-starred marriage.

"Where is Erminia, Frank?" asked his father, speaking over Maggie's shoulder, while he still held her hand. "I want to take Mrs. Browne to your mother. I told Erminia to be here to welcome this little girl."

"I'll take her to Minnie; I think she's in the garden. I'll come back to you," nodding to Edward, "directly, and then we will go to the rabbits."

So Frank and Maggie left the great lofty room, full of strange rare things, and rich with books, and went into the sunny scented garden, which stretched far and wide behind the house. Down one of the walks, with a hedge of roses on either side, came a little tripping fairy, with long golden ringlets, and a complexion like a china rose. With the deep blue of the summer sky behind her, Maggie thought she looked like an angel. She neither hastened nor slackened her pace when she saw them, but came on with the same dainty light prancing step.

"Make haste, Minnie," cried Frank.

But Minnie stopped to gather a rose.

"Don't stay with me," said Maggie, softly, although she had held his hand like that of a friend, and did not feel that the little fairy's manner was particularly cordial or gracious. Frank took her at her word, and ran off to Edward.

Erminia came a little quicker when she saw that Maggie was left alone; but for some time after they were together, they had nothing to say to each other. Erminia was easily impressed by the pomps and vanities of the world; and Maggie's new handsome frock seemed to her made of old ironed brown silk. And though Maggie's voice was soft, with a silver ringing sound in it, she pronounced her words in Nancy's broad country way. Her hair was cut short all round; her shoes were thick, and clumped as she walked. Erminia patronized her, and thought herself very kind and condescending; but they were not particularly friendly. The visit promised to be more honorable than agreeable, and Maggie almost wished herself at home again. Dinner-time came. Mrs. Buxton dined in her own room. Mr. Buxton was hearty, and jovial, and pressing; he almost scolded Maggie because she would not take more than twice of his favorite pudding: but she remembered what her mother had said, and that she would be watched all day; and this gave her a little prim, quaint manner, very different from her usual soft charming unconsciousness. She fancied that Edward and Master Buxton were just as little at their ease with each other as she and

Miss Harvey. Perhaps this feeling on the part of the boys made all four children unite after dinner.

"Let us go to the swing in the shrubbery," said Frank, after a little consideration; and off they ran. Frank proposed that he and Edward should swing the two little girls; and for a time all went on very well. But by-and-by Edward thought, that Maggie had had enough, and that he should like a turn; and Maggie, at his first word, got out.

"Don't you like swinging?" asked Erminia.

"Yes! but Edward would like it now." And Edward accordingly took her place. Frank turned away, and would not swing him. Maggie strove hard to do it, but he was heavy, and the swing bent unevenly. He scolded her for what she could not help, and at last jumped out so roughly, that the seat hit Maggie's face, and knocked her down. When she got up, her lips quivered with pain, but she did not cry; she only looked anxiously at her frock. There was a great rent across the front breadth. Then she did shed tears—tears of fright. What would her mother say?

Erminia saw her crying.

"Are you hurt?" said she, kindly. "Oh, how your check is swelled! What a rude, cross boy your brother is!"

"I did not know he was going to jump out. I am not crying because I am hurt, but because of this great rent in my nice new frock. Mamma will be so displeased."

"Is it a new frock?" asked Erminia.

"It is a new one for me. Nancy has sat up several nights to make it. Oh! what shall I do?"

Erminia's little heart was softened by such excessive poverty. A best frock made of shabby old silk! She put her arms round Maggie's neck, and said:

"Come with me; we will go to my aunt's dressing-room, and Dawson will give me some silk, and I'll help you to mend it."

"That's a kind little Minnie," said Frank. Ned had turned sulkily away. I do not think the boys were ever cordial again that day; for, as Frank said to his mother, "Ned might have said he was sorry; but he is a regular tyrant to that little brown mouse of a sister of his."

Erminia and Maggie went, with their arms round each other's necks, to Mrs. Buxton's dressing-room. The misfortune had made them friends. Mrs. Buxton lay on the sofa; so fair and white and colorless, in her muslin dressing-gown, that when Maggie first saw the lady lying with her eyes shut, her heart gave a start, for she thought she was dead. But she opened her large languid eyes, and called them to her, and listened to their story with interest.

"Dawson is at tea. Look, Minnie, in my work-box; there is some silk there. Take off your frock, my dear, and bring it here, and let me see how it can be mended."

"Aunt Buxton," whispered Erminia, "do let me give her one of my frocks. This is such an old thing."

"No, love. I'll tell you why afterwards," answered Mrs. Buxton. She looked at the rent, and arranged if nicely for the little girls to mend. Erminia helped Maggie with right good will. As they sat on the floor, Mrs. Buxton thought what a pretty contrast they made; Erminia, dazzlingly fair, with her golden ringlets, and her pale-blue frock; Maggie's little round white shoulders peeping out of her petticoat; her brown hair as glossy and smooth as the nuts that it resembled in color; her long black eye-lashes drooping over her clear smooth cheek, which would have given the idea of delicacy, but for the coral lips that spoke of perfect health: and when she glanced up, she showed long, liquid, dark-gray eyes. The deep red of the curtain behind, threw out these two little figures well.

Dawson came up. She was a grave elderly person, of whom Erminia was far more afraid than she was of her aunt; but at Mrs. Buxton's desire she finished mending the frock for Maggie.

"Mr. Buxton has asked some of your mamma's old friends to tea, as I am not able to go down. But I think, Dawson, I must have these two little girls to tea with me. Can you be very quiet, my dears; or shall you think it dull?"

They gladly accepted the invitation; and Erminia promised all sorts of fanciful promises as to quietness; and went about on her tiptoes in such a labored manner, that Mrs. Buxton begged her at last not to try and be quiet, as she made much less noise when she did not. It was the happiest part of the day to Maggie. Something in herself was so much in harmony with Mrs. Buxton's sweet, resigned gentleness, that it answered like an echo, and the two understood each other strangely well. They seemed like old friends, Maggie, who was reserved at home because no one cared to hear what she had to say, opened out, and told Erminia and Mrs. Buxton all about her way of spending her day, and described her home.

"How odd!" said Erminia. "I have ridden that way on Abdel-Kadr, and never seen your house."

"It is like the place the Sleeping Beauty lived in; people sometimes seem to go round it and round it, and never find it. But unless you follow a little sheep-track, which seems to end at a gray piece of rock, you may come within a stone's throw of the chimneys and never see them. I think you would think it so pretty. Do you ever come that way, ma'am?"

"No, love," answered Mrs. Buxton.

"But will you some time?"

"I am afraid I shall never be able to go out again," said Mrs. Buxton, in a voice which, though low, was very cheerful. Maggie thought how sad a lot was here before her; and by-and-by she took a little stool, and sat by Mrs. Buxton's sofa, and stole her hand into hers.

Mrs. Browne was in full tide of pride and happiness down stairs. Mr. Buxton had a number of jokes; which would have become dull from repetition (for he worked a merry idea threadbare before he would let if go), had if not been for his jovial blandness and good-nature. He liked to make people happy, and, as far as bodily wants went, he had a quick perception of what was required. He sat like a king (for, excepting the rector, there was not another gentleman of his standing at Combehurst), among six or seven ladies, who laughed merrily at all his sayings, and evidently thought Mrs. Browne had been highly honored in having been asked to dinner as well as to tea. In the evening, the carriage was ordered to take her as far as a carriage could go; and there was a little mysterious handshaking between her host and herself on taking leave, which made her very curious for the lights of home by which to examine a bit of rustling paper that had been put in her hand with some stammered-out words about Edward.

When every one had gone, there was a little gathering in Mrs. Buxton's dressing-room. Husband, son and niece, all came to give her their opinions on the day and the visitors.

"Good Mrs. Browne is a little tiresome," said Mr. Buxton, yawning. "Living in that moorland hole, I suppose. However, I think she has enjoyed her day; and we'll ask her down now and then, for Browne's sake. Poor Browne! What a good man he was!"

"I don't like that boy at all," said Frank. "I beg you'll not ask him again while I'm at home: he is so selfish and self-important; and yet he's a bit snobbish now and then. Mother! I know what you mean by that look. Well! if I am self-important sometimes, I'm not a snob."

"Little Maggie is very nice," said Erminia. "What a pity she has not a new frock! Was not she good about it, Frank, when she tore it?"

"Yes, she's a nice little thing enough, if she does not get all spirit cowed out of her by that brother. I'm thankful that he is going to school."

When Mrs. Browne heard where Maggie had drank tea, she was offended. She had only sat with Mrs. Buxton for an hour before dinner. If Mrs. Buxton could bear the noise of children, she could not think why she shut herself up in that room, and gave herself such airs. She supposed it was because she was the granddaughter of Sir Henry Biddulph that she took upon herself to have such whims, and not sit at the head of her table, or make tea for her company in a civil decent way. Poor Mr. Buxton! What a sad life for a merry, light-hearted man to have such a wife! It was a good thing for him to have agreeable society sometimes. She thought he looked a deal better for seeing his friends. He must be sadly moped with that sickly wife.

(If she had been clairvoyant at that moment, she might have seen Mr. Buxton tenderly chafing his wife's hands, and feeling in his innermost soul a wonder how one so saint-like could ever have learnt to love such a boor as he was; it was the wonderful mysterious blessing of his life. So little do we know of the inner truths of the households, where we come and go like intimate guests!)

Maggie could not bear to hear Mrs. Buxton spoken of as a fine lady assuming illness. Her heart beat hard as she spoke. "Mamma! I am sure she is really ill. Her lips kept going so white; and her hand was so burning hot all the time that I held it."

"Have you been holding Mrs. Buxton's hand? Where were your manners? You are a little forward creature, and ever were. But don't pretend to know better than your elders. It is no use telling me Mrs. Buxton is ill, and she able to bear the noise of children."

"I think they are all a pack of set-up people, and that Frank Buxton is the worst of all," said Edward.

Maggie's heart sank within her to hear this cold, unkind way of talking over the friends who had done so much to make their day happy. She had never before ventured into the world, and did not know how common and universal is the custom of picking to pieces those with whom we have just been associating; and so it pained her. She was a little depressed, too, with the idea that she should never see Mrs. Buxton and the lovely Erminia again. Because no future visit or intercourse had been spoken about, she fancied it would never take place; and she felt like the man in the Arabian Nights, who caught a glimpse of the precious stones and dazzling glories of the cavern, which was immediately after closed, and shut up into the semblance of hard, barren rock. She tried to recall the house. Deep blue, crimson red, warm brown draperies, were so striking after the light chintzes of her own house; and the effect of a suite of rooms opening out of each other was something quite new to the little girl; the apartments seemed to melt away into vague distance, like the dim endings of the arched aisles in church. But most of all she tried to recall Mrs. Buxton's face; and Nancy had at last to put away her work, and come to bed, in order to soothe the poor child, who was crying at the thought that Mrs. Buxton would soon die, and that she should never see her again. Nancy loved Maggie dearly, and felt no jealousy of this warm admiration of the unknown lady. She listened to her story and her fears till the sobs were hushed; and the moon fell through the casement on the white closed eyelids of one, who still sighed in her sleep.

Chapter III.

In three weeks, the day came for Edward's departure. A great cake and a parcel of gingerbread soothed his sorrows on leaving home.

"Don't cry, Maggie!" said he to her on the last morning; "you see I don't. Christmas will soon be here, and I dare say I shall find time to write to you now and then. Did Nancy put any citron in the cake?"

Maggie wished she might accompany her mother to Combehurst to see Edward off by the coach; but it was not to be. She went with them, without her bonnet, as far as her mother would allow her; and then she sat down, and watched their progress for a long, long way. She was startled by the sound of a horse's feet, softly trampling through the long heather. It was Frank Buxton's.

"My father thought Mrs. Browne would like to see the Woodchester Herald. Is Edward gone?" said he, noticing her sad face.

"Yes! he is just gone down the hill to the coach. I dare say you can see him crossing the bridge, soon. I did so want to have gone with him," answered she, looking wistfully toward the town.

Frank felt sorry for her, left alone to gaze after her brother, whom, strange as it was, she evidently regretted. After a minute's silence, he said:

"You liked riding the other day. Would you like a ride now? Rhoda is very gentle, if you can sit on my saddle. Look! I'll shorten the stirrup. There now; there's a brave little girl! I'll lead her very carefully. Why, Erminia durst not ride without a side-saddle! I'll tell you what; I'll bring the newspaper every Wednesday till I go to school, and you shall have a ride. Only I wish we had a side-saddle for Rhoda. Or, if Erminia will let me, I'll bring Abdel-Kadr, the little Shetland you rode the other day."

"But will Mr. Buxton let you?" asked Maggie, half delighted—half afraid.

"Oh, my father! to be sure he will. I have him in very good order."

Maggie was rather puzzled by this way of speaking.

"When do you go to school?" asked she.

"Toward the end of August; I don't know the day."

"Does Erminia go to school?"

"No. I believe she will soon though, if mamma does not get better." Maggie liked the change of voice, as he spoke of his mother.

"There, little lady! now jump down. Famous! you've a deal of spirit, you little brown mouse."

Nancy came out, with a wondering look, to receive Maggie.

"It is Mr. Frank Buxton," said she, by way of an introduction. "He has brought mamma the newspaper."

"Will you walk in, sir, and rest? I can tie up your horse."

"No, thank you," said he, "I must be off. Don't forget, little mousey, that you are to ready for another ride next Wednesday." And away he went.

It needed a good deal of Nancy's diplomacy to procure Maggie this pleasure; although I don't know why Mrs. Browne should have denied it, for the circle they went was always within sight of the knoll in front of the house, if any one cared enough about the matter to mount it, and look after them. Frank and Maggie got great friends in these rides. Her fearlessness delighted and surprised him, she had seemed so cowed and timid at first. But she was only so with people, as he found out before holidays ended. He saw her shrink from particular looks and inflexions of voice of her mother's; and learnt to read them, and dislike Mrs. Browne accordingly, notwithstanding all her sugary manner toward himself. The result of his observations he communicated to his mother, and in consequence, he was the bearer of a most civil and ceremonious message from Mrs. Buxton to Mrs. Browne, to the effect that the former would be much obliged to the latter if she would allow Maggie to ride down occasionally with the groom, who would bring the newspapers on the Wednesdays (now Frank was going to school), and to spend the afternoon with Erminia. Mrs. Browne consented, proud of the honor, and yet a little annoyed that no mention was made of herself. When Frank had bid good-bye, and fairly disappeared, she turned to Maggie.

"You must not set yourself up if you go among these fine folks. It is their way of showing attention to your father and myself. And you must mind and work doubly hard on Thursdays to make up for playing on Wednesdays."

Maggie was in a flush of sudden color, and a happy palpitation of her fluttering little heart. She could hardly feel any sorrow that the kind Frank was going away, so brimful was she of the thoughts of seeing his mother; who had grown strangely associated in her dreams, both sleeping and waking, with the still calm marble effigies that lay for ever clasping their hands in prayer on the altar-tombs in Combehurst church. All the week was one happy season of anticipation. She was afraid her mother was secretly irritated at her natural rejoicing; and so she did not speak to her about it, but she kept awake till Nancy came to bed, and poured into her sympathizing ears every detail, real or imaginary, of her past or future intercourse with Mrs. Buxton, and the old servant listened with interest, and fell into the custom of picturing the future with the ease and simplicity of a child.

"Suppose, Nancy! only suppose, you know, that she did die. I don't mean really die, but go into a trance like death; she looked as if she was in one when I first saw her; I would not leave her, but I would sit by her, and watch her, and watch her."

"Her lips would be always fresh and red," interrupted Nancy.

"Yes, I know you've told me before how they keep red— I should look at them quite steadily; I would try never to go to sleep."

"The great thing would be to have air-holes left in the coffin." But Nancy felt the little girl creep close to her at the grim suggestion, and, with the tact of love, she changed the subject.

"Or supposing we could hear of a doctor who could charm away illness. There were such in my young days; but I don't think people are so knowledgeable now. Peggy Jackson, that lived near us when I was a girl, was cured of a waste by a charm."

"What is a waste, Nancy?"

"It is just a pining away. Food does not nourish nor drink strengthen them, but they just fade off, and grow thinner and thinner, till their shadow looks gray instead of black at noonday; but he cured her in no time by a charm."

"Oh, if we could find him."

"Lass, he's dead, and she's dead, too, long ago!"

While Maggie was in imagination going over moor and fell, into the hollows of the distant mysterious hills, where she imagined all strange beasts and weird people to haunt, she fell asleep.

Such were the fanciful thoughts which were engendered in the little girl's mind by her secluded and solitary life. It was more solitary than ever, now that Edward was gone to school. The house missed his loud cheerful voice, and bursting presence. There seemed much less to be done, now that his numerous wants no longer called for ministration and attendance. Maggie did her task of work on her own gray rock; but as it was sooner finished, now that he was not there to interrupt and call her off, she used to stray up the Fell Lane at the back of the house; a little steep stony lane, more like stairs cut in the rock than what we, in the level land, call a lane: it reached on to the wide and open moor, and near its termination there was a knotted thorn-tree; the only tree for apparent miles. Here the sheep crouched under the storms, or stood and shaded themselves in the noontide heat. The ground was brown with their cleft round foot-marks; and tufts of wool were hung on the lower part of the stem, like votive offerings on some shrine. Here Maggie used to come and sit and dream in any scarce half-hour of leisure. Here she came to cry, when her little heart was overfull at her mother's sharp fault-finding, or when bidden to keep out of the way, and not be troublesome. She used to look over the swelling expanse of moor, and the tears were dried up by the soft low-blowing wind which came sighing along it. She forgot her little home griefs to wonder why a brown-purple shadow always streaked one particular part in the fullest sunlight; why the cloud-shadows always seemed to be wafted with a sidelong motion; or she would imagine what lay beyond those old gray holy hills, which seemed to bear up the white clouds of Heaven on which the angels flew abroad. Or she would look straight up through the quivering air, as long as she could bear its white dazzling, to try and see God's throne in that unfathomable and infinite depth of blue. She thought she should see it blaze forth sudden and glorious, if she were but full of faith. She always came down from the thorn, comforted, and meekly gentle.

But there was danger of the child becoming dreamy, and finding her pleasure in life in reverie, not in action, or endurance, or the holy rest which comes after both, and prepares for further striving or bearing. Mrs. Buxton's kindness prevented this danger just in time. It was partly out of interest in Maggie, but also partly to give Erminia a companion, that she wished the former to come down to Combehurst.

When she was on these visits, she received no regular instruction; and yet all the knowledge, and most of the strength of her character, was derived from these occasional hours. It is true her mother had given her daily lessons in reading, writing, and arithmetic; but both teacher and taught felt these more as painful duties to be gone through, than understood them as means to an end. The "There! child; now that's done with," of relief, from Mrs. Browne, was heartily echoed in Maggie's breast, as the dull routine was concluded.

Mrs. Buxton did not make a set labor of teaching; I suppose she felt that much was learned from her superintendence, but she never thought of doing or saying anything with a latent idea of its indirect effect upon the little girls, her companions. She was simply herself; she even confessed (where the confession was called for) to short-comings, to faults, and never denied the force of temptations, either of those which beset little children, or of those which occasionally assailed herself. Pure, simple, and truthful to the heart's core, her life, in its uneventful hours and days, spoke many homilies. Maggie, who was grave, imaginative, and somewhat quaint, took pains in finding words to express the thoughts to which her solitary life had given rise, secure of Mrs. Buxton's ready understanding and sympathy.

"You are so like a cloud," said she to Mrs. Buxton. "Up at the Thorn-tree, it was quite curious how the clouds used to shape themselves, just according as I was glad or sorry. I have seen the same clouds, that, when I came up first, looked like a heap of little snow-hillocks over babies' graves, turn, as soon as I grew happier, to a sort of long bright row of angels. And you seem always to have had some sorrow when I am sad, and turn bright and hopeful as soon as I grow glad. Dear Mrs. Buxton! I wish Nancy knew you."

The gay, volatile, willful, warm-hearted Erminia was less earnest in all things. Her childhood had been passed amid the distractions of wealth; and passionately bent upon the attainment of some object at one moment, the next found her angry at being reminded of the vanished anxiety she had shown but a moment before. Her life was a shattered mirror; every part dazzling and brilliant, but wanting the coherency and perfection of a whole. Mrs. Buxton strove to bring her to a sense of the beauty of completeness, and the relation which qualities and objects bear to each other; but in all her striving she retained hold of the golden clue of sympathy. She would enter into Erminia's eagerness, if the object of it varied twenty times a day; but by-and-by, in her own mild, sweet, suggestive way, she would place all these objects in their right and fitting places, as they were worthy of desire. I do not know how it was, but all discords, and disordered fragments, seemed to fall into harmony and order before her presence.

She had no wish to make the two little girls into the same kind of pattern character. They were diverse as the lily and the rose. But she tried to give stability and earnestness to Erminia; while she aimed to direct Maggie's imagination, so as to make it a great minister to high ends, instead of simply contributing to the vividness and duration of a reverie.

She told her tales of saints and martyrs, and all holy heroines, who forgot themselves, and strove only to be "ministers of Him, to do His pleasure." The tears glistened in the eyes of hearer and speaker, while she spoke in her low, faint voice, which was almost choked at times when she came to the noblest part of all.

But when she found that Maggie was in danger of becoming too little a dweller in the present, from the habit of anticipating the occasion for some great heroic action, she spoke of other heroines. She told her how, though the lives of these women of old were only known to us through some striking glorious deed, they yet must have built up the temple of their perfection by many noiseless stories; how, by small daily offerings laid on the altar, they must have obtained their beautiful strength for the crowning sacrifice. And then she would turn and speak of those whose names will never be blazoned on earth—some poor maid-servant, or hard-worked artisan, or weary governess—who have gone on through life quietly, with holy purposes in their hearts, to which they gave up pleasure and ease, in a soft, still, succession of resolute days. She quoted those lines of George Herbert's:

"All may have,
If they dare choose, a glorious life, or grave."

And Maggie's mother was disappointed because Mrs. Buxton had never offered to teach her "to play on the piano," which was to her the very head and front of a genteel education. Maggie, in all her time of yearning to become Joan of Arc, or some great heroine, was unconscious that she herself showed no little heroism, in bearing meekly what she did every day from her mother. It was hard to be questioned about Mrs. Buxton, and then to have her answers turned into subjects for contempt, and fault-finding with that sweet lady's ways.

When Ned came home for the holidays, he had much to tell. His mother listened for hours to his tales; and proudly marked all that she could note of his progress in learning. His copy-books and writing-flourishes were a sight to behold; and his account-books contained towers and pyramids of figures.

"Ay, ay!" said Mr. Buxton, when they were shown to him; "this is grand! when I was a boy I could make a flying eagle with one stroke of my pen, but I never could do all this. And yet I thought myself a fine fellow, I warrant you. And these sums! why man! I must make you my agent. I need one, I'm sure; for though I get an accountant every two or three years to do up my books, they somehow have the knack of getting wrong again. Those quarries, Mrs. Browne, which every one says are so valuable, and for the stone out of which receive orders amounting to hundreds of pounds, what d'ye think was the profit I made last year, according to my books?"

"I'm sure I don't know, sir; something very great, I've no doubt."

"Just seven-pence three farthings," said he, bursting into a fit of merry laughter, such as another man would have kept for the announcement of enormous profits. "But I must manage things differently soon. Frank will want money when he goes to Oxford, and he shall have it. I'm but a rough sort of fellow, but Frank shall take his place as a gentleman. Aha, Miss Maggie! and where's my gingerbread? There you go, creeping up to Mrs. Buxton on a Wednesday, and have never taught Cook how to make gingerbread yet. Well, Ned! and how are the classics going on? Fine fellow, that Virgil! Let me see, how does it begin?

> *'Arma, virumque cano,*
> *Trojae qui primus ab oris.'*

That's pretty well, I think, considering I've never opened him since I left school thirty years ago. To be sure, I spent six hours a day at it when I was there. Come now, I'll puzzle you. Can you construe this?

> *"Infir dealis, inoak noneis; inmud eelis, inclay noneis."*

"To be sure I can," said Edward, with a little contempt in his tone. "Can you do this, sir?

> *"Apud in is almi des ire,*
> *Mimis tres i neve require,*
> *Alo veri findit a gestis,*
> *His miseri ne ver at restis."*

But though Edward had made much progress, and gained three prizes, his moral training had been little attended to. He was more tyrannical than ever, both to his mother and Maggie. It was a drawn battle between him and Nancy, and they kept aloof from each other as much as possible. Maggie fell into her old humble way of submitting to his will, as long as it did not go against her conscience; but that, being daily enlightened by her habits of pious aspiring thought, would not allow her to be so utterly obedient as formerly. In addition to his imperiousness, he had learned to affix the idea of cleverness to various artifices and subterfuges which utterly revolted her by their meanness.

"You are so set up, by being intimate with Erminia, that you won't do a thing I tell you; you are as selfish and self-willed as"—he made a pause. Maggie was ready to cry.

"I will do anything, Ned, that is right."

"Well! and I tell you this is right."

"How can it be?" said she, sadly, almost wishing to be convinced.

"How—why it is, and that's enough for you. You must always have a reason for everything now. You are not half so nice as you were. Unless one chops logic with you, and convinces you by a long argument, you'll do nothing. Be obedient, I tell you. That is what a woman has to be."

"I could be obedient to some people, without knowing their reasons, even though they told me to do silly things," said Maggie, half to herself.

"I should like to know to whom," said Edward, scornfully.

"To Don Quixote," answered she, seriously; for, indeed, he was present in her mind just then, and his noble, tender, melancholy character had made a strong impression there.

Edward stared at her for a moment, and then burst into a loud fit of laughter. It had the good effect of restoring him to a better frame of mind. He had such an excellent joke against his sister, that he could not be angry with her. He called her Sancho Panza all the rest of the holidays, though she protested against it, saying she could not bear the Squire, and disliked being called by his name.

Frank and Edward seemed to have a mutual antipathy to each other, and the coldness between them was rather increased than diminished by all Mr. Buxton's efforts to bring them together. "Come, Frank, my lad!" said he, "don't be so stiff with Ned. His father was a dear friend of mine, and I've set my heart on seeing you friends. You'll have it in your power to help him on in the world."

But Frank answered, "He is not quite honorable, sir. I can't bear a boy who is not quite honorable. Boys brought up at those private schools are so full of tricks!"

"Nay, my lad, there thou'rt wrong. I was brought up at a private school, and no one can say I ever dirtied my hands with a trick in my life. Good old Mr. Thompson would have flogged the life out of a boy who did anything mean or underhand."

Chapter IV.

Summers and winters came and went, with little to mark them, except the growth of the trees, and the quiet progress of young creatures. Erminia was sent to school somewhere in France, to receive more regular instruction than she could have in the house with her invalid aunt. But she came home once a year, more lovely and elegant and dainty than ever; and Maggie thought, with truth, that ripening years were softening down her volatility, and that her aunt's dewlike sayings had quietly sunk deep, and fertilized the soil. That aunt was fading away. Maggie's devotion added materially to her happiness; and both she and Maggie never forgot that this devotion was to be in all things subservient to the duty which she owed to her mother.

"My love," Mrs. Buxton had more than once said, "you must always recollect that your first duty is toward your mother. You know how glad I am to see you; but I shall always understand how it is, if you do not come. She may often want you when neither you nor I can anticipate it."

Mrs. Browne had no great wish to keep Maggie at home, though she liked to grumble at her going. Still she felt that it was best, in every way, to keep on good terms with such valuable friends; and she appreciated, in some small degree, the advantage which her intimacy at the house was to Maggie. But yet she could not restrain a few complaints, nor withhold from her, on her return, a recapitulation of all the things which might have been done if she had only been at home, and the number of times that she had been wanted; but when she found that Maggie quietly gave up her next Wednesday's visit as soon as she was made aware of any necessity for her presence at home, her mother left off grumbling, and took little or no notice of her absence.

When the time came for Edward to leave school, he announced that he had no intention of taking orders, but meant to become an attorney.

"It's such slow work," said he to his mother. "One toils away for four or five years, and then one gets a curacy of seventy pounds a-year, and no end of work to do for the money. Now the work is not much harder in a lawyer's office, and if one has one's wits about one, there are hundreds and thousands a-year to be picked up with mighty little trouble."

Mrs. Browne was very sorry for this determination. She had a great desire to see her son a clergyman, like his father. She did not consider whether his character was fitted for so sacred an office; she rather thought that the profession itself, when once assumed, would purify the character; but, in fact, his fitness or unfitness for holy orders entered little into her mind. She had a respect for the profession, and his father had belonged to it.

"I had rather see you a curate at seventy pounds a-year, than an attorney with seven hundred," replied she. "And you know your father was always asked to dine everywhere—to places where I know they would not have asked Mr. Bish, of Woodchester, and he makes his thousand a-year. Besides, Mr.

Buxton has the next presentation to Combehurst, and you would stand a good chance for your father's sake. And in the mean time you should live here, if your curacy was any way near."

"I dare say! Catch me burying myself here again. My dear mother, it's a very respectable place for you and Maggie to live in, and I dare say you don't find it dull; but the idea of my quietly sitting down here is something too absurd!"

"Papa did, and was very happy," said Maggie.

"Yes! after he had been at Oxford," replied Edward, a little nonplussed by this reference to one whose memory even the most selfish and thoughtless must have held in respect.

"Well! and you know you would have to go to Oxford first."

"Maggie! I wish you would not interfere between my mother and me. I want to have it settled and done with, and that it will never be if you keep meddling. Now, mother, don't you see how much better it will be for me to go into Mr. Bish's office? Harry Bish has spoken to his father about it."

Mrs. Browne sighed.

"What will Mr. Buxton say?" asked she, dolefully.

"Say! Why don't you see it was he who first put it into my head, by telling me that first Christmas holidays, that I should be his agent. That would be something, would it not? Harry Bish says he thinks a thousand a-year might ha made of it."

His loud, decided, rapid talking overpowered Mrs. Browne; but she resigned herself to his wishes with more regrets than she had ever done before. It was not the first case in which fluent declamation has taken the place of argument.

Edward was articled to Mr. Bish, and thus gained his point. There was no one with power to resist his wishes, except his mother and Mr. Buxton. The former had long acknowledged her son's will as her law; and the latter, though surprised and almost disappointed at a change of purpose which he had never anticipated in his plans for Edward's benefit, gave his consent, and even advanced some of the money requisite for the premium.

Maggie looked upon this change with mingled feelings. She had always from a child pictured Edward to herself as taking her father's place. When she had thought of him as a man, it was as contemplative, grave, and gentle, as she remembered her father. With all a child's deficiency of reasoning power, she had never considered how impossible it was that a selfish, vain, and impatient boy could become a meek, humble, and pious man, merely by adopting a profession in which such qualities are required. But now, at sixteen, she was beginning to understand all this. Not by any process of thought, but by something more like a correct feeling, she perceived that Edward would never be the true minister of Christ. So, more glad and thankful than sorry, though sorrow mingled with her sentiments, she learned the decision that he was to be an attorney.

Frank Buxton all this time was growing up into a young man. The hopes both of father and mother were bound up in him; and, according to the difference in their characters was the difference in their hopes. It seemed, indeed, probable that Mr. Buxton, who was singularly void of worldliness or ambition for himself, would become worldly and ambitious for his son. His hopes for Frank were all for honor and distinction here. Mrs. Buxton's hopes were prayers. She was fading away, as light fades into darkness on a summer evening. No one seemed to remark the gradual progress; but she was fully conscious of it herself. The last time that Frank was at home from college before her death, she knew that she should never see him again; and when he gaily left the house, with a cheerfulness, which was partly assumed, she dragged herself with languid steps into a room at the front of the house, from which she could watch him down the long, straggling little street, that led to the inn from which the coach started. As he went along, he turned to look back at his home; and there he saw his mother's white figure gazing after him. He could not see her wistful eyes, but he made her poor heart give a leap of joy by turning round and running back for one more kiss and one more blessing.

When he next came home, it was at the sudden summons of her death.

His father was as one distracted. He could not speak of the lost angel without sudden bursts of tears, and oftentimes of self-upbraiding, which disturbed the calm, still, holy ideas, which Frank liked to associate with her. He ceased speaking to him, therefore, about their mutual loss; and it was a certain kind of relief to both when he did so; but he longed for some one to whom he might talk of his mother, with the quiet reverence of intense and trustful affection. He thought of Maggie, of whom he had seen but little of late; for when he had been at Combehurst, she had felt that Mrs. Buxton required her presence less, and had remained more at home. Possibly Mrs. Buxton regretted this; but she never said anything. She, far-looking, as one who was near death, foresaw that, probably, if Maggie and her son met often in her sick-room, feelings might arise which would militate against her husband's hopes and plans, and which, therefore, she ought not to allow to spring up. But she had been unable to refrain from expressing her gratitude to Maggie for many hours of tranquil happiness, and had unconsciously dropped many sentences which made Frank feel, that, in the little brown mouse of former years, he was likely to meet with one who could tell him much of the inner history of his mother in her last days, and to whom he could speak of her without calling out the passionate sorrow which was so little in unison with her memory.

Accordingly, one afternoon, late in the autumn, he rode up to Mrs. Browne's. The air on the heights was so still that nothing seemed to stir. Now and then a yellow leaf came floating down from the trees, detached from no outward violence, but only because its life had reached its full limit and then ceased. Looking down on the distant sheltered woods, they were gorgeous in orange and crimson, but their splendor was felt to be the sign of the decaying and dying year. Even without an inward sorrow, there was a grand solemnity in the season which impressed the mind, and hushed it into tranquil thought. Frank rode slowly along, and quietly dismounted at the old horse-mount, beside which there was an iron bridle-ring fixed in the gray stone wall. He saw the casement of the parlor-window open, and Maggie's head bent down over her work. She looked up as he entered the court, and his footsteps sounded on the flag-walk. She came round and opened the door. As she stood in the door-way, speaking, he was struck by her resemblance to some old painting. He had seen her young, calm face, shining out with great peacefulness, and the large, grave, thoughtful eyes, giving the character to the features which otherwise they might, from their very regularity, have wanted. Her brown dress had the exact tint which a painter would have admired. The slanting mellow sunlight fell upon her as she stood; and the vine-leaves, already frost-tinted, made a rich, warm border, as they hung over the old house-door.

"Mamma is not well; she is gone to lie down. How are you? How is Mr. Buxton?"

"We are both pretty well; quite well, in fact, as far as regards health. May I come in? I want to talk to you, Maggie!"

She opened the little parlor-door, and they went in; but for a time they were both silent. They could not speak of her who was with them, present in their thoughts. Maggie shut the casement, and put a log of wood on the fire. She sat down with her back to the window; but as the flame sprang up, and blazed at the touch of the dry wood, Frank saw that her face was wet with quiet tears. Still her voice was even and gentle, as she answered his questions. She seemed to understand what were the very things he would care most to hear. She spoke of his mother's last days; and without any word of praise (which, indeed, would have been impertinence), she showed such a just and true appreciation of her who was dead and gone, that he felt as if he could listen forever to the sweet-dropping words. They were balm to his sore heart. He had thought it possible that the suddenness of her death might have made her life incomplete, in that she might have departed without being able to express wishes and projects, which would now have the sacred force of commands. But he found that Maggie, though she had never intruded herself as such, had been the depository of many little thoughts and plans; or, if they were not expressed to her, she knew that Mr. Buxton or Dawson was aware of what they were, though, in their violence of early grief, they had forgotten to name them. The flickering brightness of the flame had died away; the gloom of evening had gathered into the room, through the open door of which the kitchen fire sent a ruddy glow, distinctly marked against carpet and wall. Frank still sat, with his head buried in his hands against the table, listening.

"Tell me more," he said, at every pause.

"I think I have told you all now," said Maggie, at last. "At least, it is all I recollect at present; but if I think of anything more, I will be sure and tell you."

"Thank you; do." He was silent for some time.

"Erminia is coming home at Christmas. She is not to go back to Paris again. She will live with us. I hope you and she will be great friends, Maggie."

"Oh yes," replied she. "I think we are already. At least we were last Christmas. You know it is a year since I have seen her."

"Yes; she went to Switzerland with Mademoiselle Michel, instead of coming home the last time. Maggie, I must go, now. My father will be waiting dinner for me."

"Dinner! I was going to ask if you would not stay to tea. I hear mamma stirring about in her room. And Nancy is getting things ready, I see. Let me go and tell mamma. She will not be pleased unless she sees you. She has been very sorry for you all," added she, dropping her voice.

Before he could answer, she ran up stairs.

Mrs. Browne came down.

"Oh, Mr. Frank! Have you been sitting in the dark? Maggie, you ought to have rung for candles! Ah! Mr. Frank, you've had a sad loss since I saw you here—let me see—in the last week of September. But she was always a sad invalid; and no doubt your loss is her gain. Poor Mr. Buxton, too! How is he? When one thinks of him, and of her years of illness, it seems like a happy release."

She could have gone on for any length of time, but Frank could not bear this ruffling up of his soothed grief, and told her that his father was expecting him home to dinner.

"Ah! I am sure you must not disappoint him. He'll want a little cheerful company more than ever now. You must not let him dwell on it, Mr. Frank, but turn his thoughts another way by always talking of other things. I am sure if I had some one to speak to me in a cheerful, pleasant way, when poor dear Mr. Browne died, I should never have fretted after him as I did; but the children were too young, and there was no one to come and divert me with any news. If I'd been living in Combehurst, I am sure I should not have let my grief get the better of me as I did. Could you get up a quiet rubber in the evenings, do you think?"

But Frank had shaken hands and was gone. As he rode home he thought much of sorrow, and the different ways of bearing it. He decided that it was sent by God for some holy purpose, and to call out into existence some higher good; and he thought that if it were faithfully taken as His decree there would be no passionate, despairing resistance to it; nor yet, if it were trustfully acknowledged to have some wise end, should we dare to baulk it, and defraud it by putting it on one side, and, by seeking the distractions of worldly things, not let it do its full work. And then he returned to his conversation with Maggie. That had been real comfort to him. What an advantage it would be to Erminia to have such a girl for a friend and companion!

It was rather strange that, having this thought, and having been struck, as I said, with Maggie's appearance while she stood in the door-way (and I may add that this impression of her unobtrusive beauty had been deepened by several succeeding interviews), he should reply as he did to Erminia's remark, on first seeing Maggie after her return from France.

"How lovely Maggie is growing! Why, I had no idea she would ever turn out pretty. Sweet-looking she always was; but now her style of beauty makes her positively distinguished. Frank! speak! is not she beautiful?"

"Do you think so?" answered he, with a kind of lazy indifference, exceedingly gratifying to his father, who was listening with some eagerness to his answer. That day, after dinner, Mr. Buxton began to ask his opinion of Erminia's appearance.

Frank answered at once:

"She is a dazzling little creature. Her complexion looks as if it were made of cherries and milk; and, it must be owned, the little lady has studied the art of dress to some purpose in Paris."

Mr. Buxton was nearer happiness at this reply than he had ever been since his wife's death; for the only way he could devise to satisfy his reproachful conscience towards his neglected and unhappy sister, was to plan a marriage between his son and her child. He rubbed his hands and drank two extra glasses of wine.

"We'll have the Brownes to dinner, as usual, next Thursday," said he, "I am sure your mother would have been hurt if we had omitted it; it is now nine years since they began to come, and they have never missed one Christmas since. Do you see any objection, Frank?"

"None at all, sir," answered he. "I intend to go up to town soon after Christmas, for a week or ten days, on my way to Cambridge. Can I do anything for you?"

"Well, I don't know. I think I shall go up myself some day soon. I can't understand all these lawyer's letters, about the purchase of the Newbridge estate; and I fancy I could make more sense out of it all, if I saw Mr. Hodgson."

"I wish you would adopt my plan, of having an agent, sir. Your affairs are really so complicated now, that they would take up the time of an expert man of business. I am sure all those tenants at Dumford ought to be seen after."

"I do see after them. There's never a one that dares cheat me, or that would cheat me if they could. Most of them have lived under the Buxtons for generations. They know that if they dared to take advantage of me, I should come down upon them pretty smartly."

"Do you rely upon their attachment to your family—or on their idea of your severity?"

"On both. They stand me instead of much trouble in account-keeping, and those eternal lawyers' letters some people are always dispatching to their tenants. When I'm cheated, Frank, I give you leave to make me have an agent, but not till then. There's my little Erminia singing away, and nobody to hear her."

Chapter V.

Christmas-Day was strange and sad. Mrs. Buxton had always contrived to be in the drawing-room, ready to receive them all after dinner. Mr. Buxton tried to do away with his thoughts of her by much talking; but every now and then he looked wistfully toward the door. Erminia exerted herself to be as lively as she could, in order, if possible, to fill up the vacuum. Edward, who had come over from Woodchester for a walk, had a good deal to say; and was, unconsciously, a great assistance with his never-ending flow of rather clever small-talk. His mother felt proud of her son, and his new waistcoat, which was far more conspicuously of the latest fashion than Frank's could be said to be. After dinner, when Mr. Buxton and the two young men were left alone, Edward launched out still more. He thought he was impressing Frank with his knowledge of the world, and the world's ways. But he was doing all in his power to repel one who had never been much attracted toward him. Worldly success was his standard of merit. The end seemed with him to justify the means; if a man prospered, if was not necessary to scrutinize his conduct too closely. The law was viewed in its lowest aspect; and yet with a certain cleverness, which preserved Edward from being intellectually contemptible. Frank had entertained some idea of studying for a barrister himself: not so much as a means of livelihood as to gain some idea of the code which makes and shows a nation's conscience: but Edward's details of the ways in which the letter so often baffles the spirit, made him recoil. With some anger against himself, for viewing the profession with disgust, because it was degraded by those who embraced it, instead of looking upon it as what might be ennobled and purified into a vast intelligence by high and pure-minded men, he got up abruptly and left the room.

The girls were sitting over the drawing-room fire, with unlighted candles on the table, talking, he felt, about his mother; but when he came in they rose, and changed their tone. Erminia went to the piano, and sang her newest and choicest French airs. Frank was gloomy and silent; but when she changed into more solemn music his mood was softened, Maggie's simple and hearty admiration, untinged by the slightest shade of envy for Erminia's accomplishments, charmed him. The one appeared to him the perfection of elegant art, the other of graceful nature. When he looked at Maggie, and thought of the moorland home from which she had never wandered, the mysteriously beautiful lines of Wordsworth seemed to become sun-clear to him.

> "And she shall lean her ear
> In many a secret place
> Where rivulets dance their wayward round,
> And beauty born of murmuring sound
> Shall pass into her face."

Mr. Buxton, in the dining-room, was really getting to take an interest in Edward's puzzling cases. They were like tricks at cards. A quick motion, and out of the unpromising heap, all confused together, presto! the right card turned up. Edward stated his case, so that there did not seem loophole for the desired verdict; but through some conjuration, it always came uppermost at last. He had a graphic way of relating things; and, as he did not spare epithets in his designation of the opposing party, Mr. Buxton took it upon trust that the defendant or the prosecutor (as it might happen) was a "pettifogging knave," or a "miserly curmudgeon," and rejoiced accordingly in the triumph over him gained by the ready wit of "our governor," Mr. Bish. At last he became so deeply impressed with Edward's knowledge of law, as to consult him about some cottage property he had in Woodchester.

"I rather think there are twenty-one cottages, and they don't bring me in four pounds a-year; and out of that I have to pay for collecting. Would there be any chance of selling them? They are in Doughty-street; a bad neighborhood, I fear."

"Very bad," was Edward's prompt reply. "But if you are really anxious to effect a sale, I have no doubt I could find a purchaser in a short time."

"I should be very much obliged to you," said Mr. Buxton. "You would be doing me a kindness. If you meet with a purchaser, and can manage the affair, I would rather that you drew out the deeds for the transfer of the property. If would be the beginning of business for you; and I only hope I should bring you good luck."

Of course Edward could do this; and when they left the table, it was with a feeling on his side that he was a step nearer to the agency which he coveted; and with a happy consciousness on Mr. Buxton's of having put a few pounds in the way of a deserving and remarkably clever young man.

Since Edward had left home, Maggie had gradually, but surely, been gaining in importance. Her judgment and her untiring unselfishness could not fail to make way. Her mother had some respect for, and great dependence on her; but still it was hardly affection that she felt for her; or if it was it was a dull and torpid kind of feeling, compared with the fond love and exulting pride which she took in Edward. When he came back for occasional holidays, his mother's face was radiant with happiness, and her manner toward him was even more caressing than he approved of. When Maggie saw him repel the hand that fain would have stroked his hair as in childish days, a longing came into her heart for some of these uncared-for tokens of her mother's love. Otherwise she meekly sank back into her old secondary place, content to have her judgment slighted and her wishes unasked as long as he stayed. At times she was now beginning to disapprove and regret some things in him; his flashiness of manner jarred against her taste; and a deeper, graver feeling was called out by his evident want of quick moral perception. "Smart and clever," or "slow and dull," took with him the place of "right and wrong." Little as he thought it, he was himself narrow-minded and dull; slow and blind to perceive the beauty and eternal wisdom of simple goodness.

Erminia and Maggie became great friends. Erminia used to beg for Maggie, until she herself put a stop to the practice; as she saw her mother yielded more frequently than was convenient, for the honor of having her daughter a visitor at Mr. Buxton's, about which she could talk to her few acquaintances who persevered in calling at the cottage. Then Erminia volunteered a visit of some days to Maggie, and Mrs. Browne's pride was redoubled; but she made so many preparations, and so much fuss, and gave herself so much trouble, that she was positively ill during Erminia's stay; and Maggie felt that she must henceforward deny herself the pleasure of having her friend for a guest, as her mother could not be persuaded from attempting to provide things in the same abundance and style as that to which Erminia was accustomed at home; whereas, as Nancy shrewdly observed, the young lady did not know if she was eating jelly, or porridge, or whether the plates were common delf or the best China, so long as she was with her dear Miss Maggie. Spring went, and summer came. Frank had gone to and fro between Cambridge and Combehurst, drawn by motives of which he felt the force, but into which he did not care to examine. Edward had sold the property of Mr. Buxton; and he, pleased with the possession of half the purchase money (the remainder of which was to be paid by installments), and happy in the idea that his son came over so frequently to see Erminia, had amply rewarded the young attorney for his services.

One summer's day, as hot as day could be, Maggie had been busy all morning; for the weather was so sultry that she would not allow either Nancy or her mother to exert themselves much. She had gone down with the old brown pitcher, coeval with herself, to the spring for water; and while it was trickling, and making a tinkling music, she sat down on the ground. The air was so still that she heard the distant wood-pigeons cooing; and round about her the bees were murmuring busily among the clustering heath. From some little touch of sympathy with these low sounds of pleasant harmony, she began to try and hum some of Erminia's airs. She never sang out loud, or put words to her songs; but her voice was very sweet, and it was a great pleasure to herself to let it go into music. Just as her jug was filled, she was startled by Frank's sudden appearance. She thought he was at Cambridge, and, from some cause or other, her face, usually so faint in color, became the most vivid scarlet. They were both too conscious to speak. Maggie stooped (murmuring some words of surprise) to take up her pitcher.

"Don't go yet, Maggie," said he, putting his hand on hers to stop her; but, somehow, when that purpose was effected, he forgot to take it off again. "I have come all the way from Cambridge to see you. I could not bear suspense any longer. I grew so impatient for certainty of some kind, that I went up to town last night, in order to feel myself on my way to you, even though I knew I could not be here a bit earlier to-day for doing so. Maggie—dear Maggie! how you are trembling! Have I frightened you? Nancy told me you were here; but it was very thoughtless to come so suddenly upon you."

It was not the suddenness of his coming; it was the suddenness of her own heart, which leaped up with the feelings called out by his words. She went very white, and sat down on the ground as before. But she rose again immediately, and stood, with drooping, averted head. He had dropped her hand, but now sought to take it again.

"Maggie, darling, may I speak?" Her lips moved, he saw, but he could not hear. A pang of affright ran through him that, perhaps, she did not wish to listen. "May I speak to you?" he asked again, quite timidly. She tried to make her voice sound, but it would not; so she looked round. Her soft gray eyes were eloquent in that one glance. And, happier than his words, passionate and tender as they were, could tell, he spoke till her trembling was changed into bright flashing blushes, and even a shy smile hovered about her lips, and dimpled her cheeks.

The water bubbled over the pitcher unheeded. At last she remembered all the work-a-day world. She lifted up the jug, and would have hurried home, but Frank decidedly took it from her.

"Henceforward," said he, "I have a right to carry your burdens." So with one arm round her waist and with the other carrying the water, they climbed the steep turfy slope. Near the top she wanted to take it again.

"Mamma will not like it. Mamma will think if so strange."

"Why, dearest, if I saw Nancy carrying it up this slope I would take it from her. It would be strange if a man did not carry it for any woman. But you must let me tell your mother of my right to help you. If is your dinner-time is it not? I may come in to dinner as one of the family may not I Maggie?"

"No" she said softly. For she longed to be alone; and she dreaded being overwhelmed by the expression of her mother's feelings, weak and agitated as she felt herself. "Not to-day."

"Not to-day!" said he reproachfully. "You are very hard upon me. Let me come to tea. If you will, I will leave you now. Let me come to early tea. I must speak to my father. He does not know I am here. I may come to tea. At what time is it? Three o'clock. Oh, I know you drink tea at some strange early hour; perhaps it is at two. I will take care to be in time."

"Don't come till five, please. I must tell mamma; and I want some time to think. It does seem so like a dream. Do go, please."

"Well! if I must, I must. But I don't feel as if I were in a dream, but in some real blessed heaven so long as I see you."

At last he went. Nancy was awaiting Maggie, the side-gate.

"Bless us and save us, bairn! what a time it has taken thee to get the water. Is the spring dry with the hot weather?"

Maggie ran past her. All dinner-time she heard her mother's voice in long-continued lamentation about something. She answered at random, and startled her mother by asserting that she thought "it" was very good; the said "it" being milk turned sour by thunder. Mrs. Browne spoke quite sharply, "No one is so particular as you, Maggie. I have known you drink water, day after day, for breakfast, when you were a little girl, because your cup of milk had a drowned fly in it; and now you tell me you don't care for this, and don't mind that, just as if you could eat up all the things which are spoiled by the heat. I declare my head aches so, I shall go and lie down as soon as ever dinner is over."

If this was her plan, Maggie thought she had no time to lose in making her confession. Frank would be here before her mother got up again to tea. But she dreaded speaking about her happiness; it seemed as yet so cobweb-like, as if a touch would spoil its beauty.

"Mamma, just wait a minute. Just sit down in your chair while I tell you something. Please, dear mamma." She took a stool, and sat at her mother's feet; and then she began to turn the wedding-ring on Mrs. Browne's hand, looking down and never speaking, till the latter became impatient.

"What is if you have got to say, child? Do make haste, for I want to go up-stairs."

With a great jerk of resolution, Maggie said:

"Mamma, Frank Buxton has asked me to marry him."

She hid her face in her mother's lap for an instant; and then she lifted it up, as brimful of the light of happiness as is the cup of a water-lily of the sun's radiance.

"Maggie—you don't say so," said her mother, half incredulously. "It can't be, for he's at Cambridge, and it's not post-day. What do you mean?"

"He came this morning, mother, when I was down at the well; and we fixed that I was to speak to you; and he asked if he might come again for tea."

"Dear! dear! and the milk all gone sour? We should have had milk of our own, if Edward had not persuaded me against buying another cow."

"I don't think Mr. Buxton will mind it much," said Maggie, dimpling up, as she remembered, half unconsciously, how little he had seemed to care for anything but herself.

"Why, what a thing it is for you!" said Mrs. Browne, quite roused up from her languor and her head-ache. "Everybody said he was engaged to Miss Erminia. Are you quite sure you made no mistake, child? What did he say? Young men are so fond of making fine speeches; and young women are so silly in fancying they mean something. I once knew a girl who thought that a gentleman who sent her mother a present of a sucking-pig, did it as a delicate way of making her an offer. Tell me his exact words."

But Maggie blushed, and either would not or could not. So Mrs. Browne began again:

"Well, if you're sure, you're sure. I wonder how he brought his father round. So long as he and Erminia have been planned for each other! That very first day we ever dined there after your father's death, Mr. Buxton as good as told me all about it. I fancied they were only waiting till they were out of mourning."

All this was news to Maggie. She had never thought that either Erminia or Frank was particularly fond of the other; still less had she had any idea of Mr. Buxton's plans for them. Her mother's surprise at her engagement jarred a little upon her too: it had become so natural, even in these last two hours, to feel that she belonged to *him*. But there were more discords to come. Mrs. Browne began again, half in soliloquy:

"I should think he would have four thousand a-year. He did not tell you, love, did he, if they had still that bad property in the canal, that his father complained about? But he will have four thousand. Why, you'll have your carriage, Maggie. Well! I hope Mr. Buxton has taken it kindly, because he'll have a deal to do with the settlements. I'm sure I thought he was engaged to Erminia."

Ringing changes on these subjects all the afternoon, Mrs. Browne sat with Maggie. She occasionally wandered off to speak about Edward, and how favorably his future prospects would be advanced by the engagement.

"Let me see—there's the house in Combehurst: the rent of that would be a hundred and fifty a-year, but we'll not reckon that. But there's the quarries" (she was reckoning upon her fingers in default of a slate, for which she had vainly searched), "we'll call them two hundred a-year, for I don't believe Mr. Buxton's stories about their only bringing him in seven-pence; and there's Newbridge, that's certainly thirteen hundred—where had I got to, Maggie?"

"Dear mamma, do go and lie down for a little; you look quite flushed," said Maggie, softly.

Was this the manner to view her betrothal with such a man as Frank? Her mother's remarks depressed her more than she could have thought it possible; the excitement of the morning was having its reaction, and she longed to go up to the solitude under the thorn-tree, where she had hoped to spend a quiet, thoughtful afternoon.

Nancy came in to replace glasses and spoons in the cupboard. By some accident, the careful old servant broke one of the former. She looked up quickly at her mistress, who usually visited all such offences with no small portion of rebuke.

"Never mind, Nancy," said Mrs. Browne. "It's only an old tumbler; and Maggie's going to be married, and we must buy a new set for the wedding-dinner."

Nancy looked at both, bewildered; at last a light dawned into her mind, and her face looked shrewdly and knowingly back at Mrs. Browne. Then she said, very quietly:

"I think I'll take the next pitcher to the well myself, and try my luck. To think how sorry I was for Miss Maggie this morning! 'Poor thing,' says I to myself, 'to be kept all this time at that confounded well' (for I'll not deny that I swear a bit to myself at times—it sweetens the blood), 'and she so tired.' I e'en thought I'd go help her; but I reckon she'd some other help. May I take a guess at the young man?"

"Four thousand a-year! Nancy;" said Mrs. Browne, exultingly.

"And a blithe look, and a warm, kind heart—and a free step—and a noble way with him to rich and poor—aye, aye, I know the name. No need to alter all my neat M.B.'s, done in turkey-red cotton. Well, well! every one's turn comes sometime, but mine's rather long a-coming."

The faithful old servant came up to Maggie, and put her hand caressingly on her shoulder. Maggie threw her arms round her neck, and kissed the brown, withered face.

"God bless thee, bairn," said Nancy, solemnly. It brought the low music of peace back into the still recesses of Maggie's heart. She began to look out for her lover; half-hidden behind the muslin window curtain, which waved gently to and fro in the afternoon breezes. She heard a firm, buoyant step, and had only time to catch one glimpse of his face, before moving away. But that one glance made her think that the hours which had elapsed since she saw him had not been serene to him any more than to her.

When he entered the parlor, his face was glad and bright. He went up in a frank, rejoicing way to Mrs. Browne; who was evidently rather puzzled how to receive him—whether as

Maggie's betrothed, or as the son of the greatest man of her acquaintance.

"I am sure, sir," said she, "we are all very much obliged to you for the honor you have done our family!"

He looked rather perplexed as to the nature of the honor which he had conferred without knowing it; but as the light dawned upon him, he made answer in a frank, merry way, which was yet full of respect for his future mother-in-law:

"And I am sure I am truly grateful for the honor one of your family has done me."

When Nancy brought in tea she was dressed in her fine-weather Sunday gown; the first time it had ever been worn out of church, and the walk to and fro.

After tea, Frank asked Maggie if she would walk out with him; and accordingly they climbed the Fell-Lane and went out upon the moors, which seemed vast and boundless as their love.

"Have you told your father?" asked Maggie; a dim anxiety lurking in her heart.

"Yes," said Frank. He did not go on; and she feared to ask, although she longed to know, how Mr. Buxton had received the intelligence.

"What did he say?" at length she inquired.

"Oh! it was evidently a new idea to him that I was attached to you; and he does not take up a new idea speedily. He has had some notion, it seems, that Erminia and I were to make a match of it; but she and I agreed, when we talked it over, that we should never have fallen in love with each other if there had not been another human being in the world. Erminia is a little sensible creature, and says she does not wonder at any man falling in love with you. Nay, Maggie, don't hang your head so down; let me have a glimpse of your face."

"I am sorry your father does not like it," said Maggie, sorrowfully.

"So am I. But we must give him time to get reconciled. Never fear but he will like it in the long run; he has too much good taste and good feeling. He must like you."

Frank did not choose to tell even Maggie how violently his father had set himself against their engagement. He was surprised and annoyed at first to find how decidedly his father was possessed with the idea that he was to marry his cousin, and that she, at any rate, was attached to him, whatever his feelings might be toward her; but after he had gone frankly to Erminia and told her all, he found that she was as ignorant of her uncle's plans for her as he had been; and almost as glad at any event which should frustrate them.

Indeed she came to the moorland cottage on the following day, after Frank had returned to Cambridge. She had left her horse in charge of the groom, near the fir-trees on the heights, and came running down the slope in her habit. Maggie went out to meet her, with just a little wonder at her heart if what Frank had said could possibly be true; and that Erminia, living in the house with him, could have remained indifferent to him. Erminia threw her arms round her neck, and they sat down together on the court-steps.

"I durst not ride down that hill; and Jem is holding my horse, so I may not stay very long; now begin, Maggie, at once, and go into a rhapsody about Frank. Is not he a charming fellow? Oh! I am so glad. Now don't sit smiling and blushing there to yourself; but tell me a great deal about it. I have so wanted to know somebody that was in love, that I might hear what it was like; and the minute I could, I came off here. Frank is only just gone. He has had another long talk with my uncle, since he came back from you this morning; but I am afraid he has not made much way yet."

Maggie sighed. "I don't wonder at his not thinking me good enough for Frank.

"No! the difficulty would be to find any one he did think fit for his paragon of a son."

"He thought you were, dearest Erminia."

"So Frank has told you that, has he? I suppose we shall have no more family secrets now," said Erminia, laughing. "But I can assure you I had a strong rival in lady Adela Castlemayne, the Duke of Wight's daughter; she was the most beautiful lady my uncle had ever seen (he only saw her in the Grand Stand at Woodchester races, and never spoke a word to her in his life). And if she would have had Frank, my uncle would still have been dissatisfied as long as the Princess Victoria was unmarried; none would have been good enough while a better remained. But Maggie," said she, smiling up into her friend's face, "I think it would have made you laugh, for all you look as if a kiss would shake the tears out of your eyes, if you could have seen my uncle's manner to me all day. He will have it that I am suffering from an unrequited attachment; so he watched me and watched me over breakfast; and at last, when I had eaten a whole nest-full of eggs, and I don't know how many pieces of toast, he rang the bell and asked for some potted charr. I was quite unconscious that it was for me, and I did not want it when it came; so he sighed in a most melancholy manner, and said, 'My poor Erminia!' If Frank had not been there, and looking dreadfully miserable, I am sure I should have laughed out."

"Did Frank look miserable?" said Maggie, anxiously.

"There now! you don't care for anything but the mention of his name."

"But did he look unhappy?" persisted Maggie.

"I can't say he looked happy, dear Mousey; but it was quite different when he came back from seeing you. You know you always had the art of stilling any person's trouble. You and my aunt Buxton are the only two I ever knew with that gift."

"I am so sorry he has any trouble to be stilled," said Maggie.

"And I think it will do him a world of good. Think how successful his life has been! the honors he got at Eton! his picture taken, and I don't know what! and at Cambridge just the same way of going on. He would be insufferably imperious in a few years, if he did not meet with a few crosses."

"Imperious!—oh Erminia, how can you say so?"

"Because it's the truth. He happens to have very good dispositions; and therefore his strong will is not either disagreeable, or offensive; but once let him become possessed by a wrong wish, and you would then see how vehement and imperious he would be. Depend upon it, my uncle's resistance is a capital thing for him. As dear sweet Aunt Buxton would have said, 'There is a holy purpose in it;' and as Aunt Buxton would not have said, but as I, a 'fool, rush in where angels fear to tread,' I decide that the purpose is to teach Master Frank patience and submission."

"Erminia—how could you help"—and there Maggie stopped.

"I know what you mean; how could I help falling in love with him? I think he has not mystery and reserve enough for me. I should like a man with some deep, impenetrable darkness around him; something one could always keep wondering about. Besides, think what clashing of wills there would have been! My uncle was very short-sighted in his plan; but I don't think he thought so much about the fitness of our characters and ways, as the fitness of our fortunes!"

"For shame, Erminia! No one cares less for money than Mr. Buxton!"

"There's a good little daughter-in-law elect! But seriously, I do think he is beginning to care for money; not in the least for himself, but as a means of aggrandizement for Frank. I have observed, since I came home at Christmas, a growing anxiety to make the most of his property; a thing he never cared about before. I don't think he is aware of it himself, but from one or two little things I have noticed, I should not wonder if he ends in being avaricious in his old age." Erminia sighed.

Maggie had almost a sympathy with the father, who sought what he imagined to be for the good of his son, and that son, Frank. Although she was as convinced as Erminia, that money could not really help any one to happiness, she could not at the instant resist saying:

"Oh! how I wish I had a fortune! I should so like to give it all to him."

"Now Maggie! don't be silly! I never heard you wish for anything different from what *was* before, so I shall take this opportunity of lecturing you on your folly. No! I won't either, for you look sadly tired with all your agitation; and besides I must go, or Jem will be wondering what has become of me. Dearest cousin-in-law, I shall come very often to see you; and perhaps I shall give you my lecture yet."

Chapter VI.

It was true of Mr. Buxton, as well as of his son, that he had the seeds of imperiousness in him. His life had not been such as to call them out into view. With more wealth than he required; with a gentle wife, who if she ruled him never showed it, or was conscious of the fact herself; looked up to by his neighbors, a simple affectionate set of people, whose fathers had lived near his father and grandfather in the same kindly relation, receiving benefits cordially given, and requiting them with good will and respectful attention: such had been the circumstances surrounding him; and until his son grew out of childhood, there had not seemed a wish which he had it not in his power to gratify as soon as formed. Again, when Frank was at school and at college, all went on prosperously; he gained honors enough to satisfy a far more ambitious father. Indeed, it was the honors he gained that stimulated his father's ambition. He received letters from tutors, and headmasters, prophesying that, if Frank chose, he might rise to the "highest honors in church or state;" and the idea thus suggested, vague as it was, remained, and filled Mr. Buxton's mind; and, for the first time in his life, made him wish that his own career had been such as would have led him to form connections among the great and powerful. But, as it was, his shyness and *gêne*, from being unaccustomed to society, had made him averse to Frank's occasional requests that he might bring such and such a school-fellow, or college-chum, home on a visit. Now he regretted this, on account of the want of those connections which might thus have been formed; and, in his visions, he turned to marriage as the best way of remedying this. Erminia was right in saying that her uncle had thought of Lady Adela Castlemayne for an instant; though how the little witch had found it out I cannot say, as the idea had been dismissed immediately from his mind.

He was wise enough to see its utter vanity, as long as his son remained undistinguished. But his hope was this. If Frank married Erminia, their united property (she being her father's heiress) would justify him in standing for the shire; or if he could marry the daughter of some leading personage in the county, it might lead to the same step; and thus at once he would obtain a position in parliament, where his great talents would have scope and verge enough. Of these two visions, the favorite one (for his sister's sake) was that of marriage with Erminia.

And, in the midst of all this, fell, like a bombshell, the intelligence of his engagement with Maggie Browne; a good sweet little girl enough, but without fortune or connection— without, as far as Mr. Buxton knew, the least power, or capability, or spirit, with which to help Frank on in his career to eminence in the land! He resolved to consider if as a boyish fancy, easily to be suppressed; and pooh-poohed it down, to Frank, accordingly. He remarked his son's set lips, and quiet determined brow, although he never spoke in a more respectful tone, than while thus steadily opposing his father. If he had shown more violence of manner, he would have irritated him less; but, as it was, if was the most miserable interview that had ever taken place between the father and son.

Mr. Buxton tried to calm himself down with believing that Frank would change his mind, if he saw more of the world; but, somehow, he had a prophesying distrust of this idea internally. The worst was, there was no fault to be found with Maggie herself, although she might want the accomplishments he desired to see in his son's wife. Her connections, too, were so perfectly respectable (though humble enough in comparison with Mr. Buxton's soaring wishes), that there was nothing to be objected to on that score; her position was the great offence. In proportion to his want of any reason but this one, for disapproving of the engagement, was his annoyance under it. He assumed a reserve toward Frank; which was so unusual a restraint upon his open, genial disposition, that it seemed to make him irritable toward all others in contact with him, excepting Erminia. He found it difficult to behave rightly to Maggie. Like all habitually cordial persons, he went into the opposite extreme, when he wanted to show a little coolness. However angry he might be with the events of which she was the cause, she was too innocent and meek to justify him in being more than cool; but his awkwardness was so great, that many a man of the world has met his greatest enemy, each knowing the other's hatred, with less freezing distance of manner than Mr. Buxton's to Maggie. While she went simply on in her own path, loving him the more through all, for old kindness' sake, and because he was Frank's father, he shunned meeting her with such evident and painful anxiety, that at last she tried to spare him the encounter, and hurried out of church, or lingered behind all, in order to avoid the only chance they now had of being forced to speak; for she no longer went to the dear house in Combehurst, though Erminia came to see her more than ever.

Mrs. Browne was perplexed and annoyed beyond measure. She upbraided Mr. Buxton to every one but Maggie. To her she said—"Any one in their senses might have foreseen what had happened, and would have thought well about it, before they went and fell in love with a young man of such expectations as Mr. Frank Buxton."

In the middle of all this dismay, Edward came over from Woodchester for a day or two. He had been told of the engagement, in a letter from Maggie herself; but if was too sacred a subject for her to enlarge upon to him; and Mrs. Browne was no letter writer. So this was his first greeting to Maggie; after kissing her:

"Well, Sancho, you've done famously for yourself. As soon as I got your letter I said to Harry Bish—'Still waters run deep; here's my little sister Maggie, as quiet a creature as ever lived, has managed to catch young Buxton, who has five thousand a-year if he's a penny.' Don't go so red, Maggie. Harry was sure to hear of if soon from some one, and I see no use in keeping it secret, for it gives consequence to us all."

"Mr. Buxton is quite put out about it," said Mrs. Brown, querulously; "and I'm sure he need not be, for he's enough of money, if that's what he wants; and Maggie's father was a clergyman, and I've seen 'yeoman,' with my own eyes, on old Mr. Buxton's (Mr. Lawrence's father's) carts; and a clergyman is above a yeoman any day. But if Maggie had had any thought for other people, she'd never have gone and engaged herself, when she might have been sure it would give offence. We are never asked down to dinner now. I've never broken bread there since last Christmas."

"Whew!" said Edward to this. It was a disappointed whistle; but he soon cheered up. "I thought I could have lent a hand in screwing old Buxton up about the settlements; but I see it's not come to that yet. Still I'll go and see the old gentleman. I'm a bit of a favorite of his, and I doubt I can turn him round."

"Pray, Edward, don't go," said Maggie. "Frank and I are content to wait; and I'm sure we would rather not have any one speak to Mr. Buxton, upon a subject which evidently gives him so much pain; please, Edward, don't!"

"Well, well. Only I must go about this property of his. Besides, I don't mean to get into disgrace; so I shan't seem to know anything about it, if it would make him angry. I want to keep on good terms, because of the agency. So, perhaps, I shall shake my head, and think it great presumption in you, Maggie, to have thought of becoming his daughter-in-law. If I can do you no good, I may as well do myself some."

"I hope you won't mention me at all," she replied.

One comfort (and almost the only one arising from Edward's visit) was, that she could now often be spared to go up to the thorn-tree, and calm down her anxiety, and bring all discords into peace, under the sweet influences of nature. Mrs. Buxton had tried to teach her the force of the lovely truth, that the "melodies of the everlasting chime" may abide in the hearts of those who ply their daily task in towns, and crowded populous places; and that solitude is not needed by the faithful for them to feel the immediate presence of God; nor utter stillness of human sound necessary, before they can hear the music of His angels' footsteps; but, as yet, her soul was a young disciple; and she felt it easier to speak to Him, and come to Him for help, sitting lonely, with wild moors swelling and darkening around her, and not a creature in sight but the white specks of distant sheep, and the birds that shun the haunts of men, floating in the still mid-air.

She sometimes longed to go to Mr. Buxton and tell him how much she could sympathize with him, if his dislike to her engagement arose from thinking her unworthy of his son. Frank's character seemed to her grand in its promise. With vehement impulses and natural gifts, craving worthy employment, his will sat supreme over all, like a young emperor calmly seated on his throne, whose fiery generals and wise counsellors stand alike ready to obey him. But if marriage were to be made by due measurement and balance of character, and if others, with their scales, were to be the judges, what would become of all the beautiful services rendered by the loyalty of true love? Where would be the raising up of the weak by the strong? or the patient endurance? or the gracious trust of her:

> *"Whose faith is fixt and cannot move;*
> *She darkly feels him great and wise,*
> *She dwells on him with faithful eyes,*
> *'I cannot understand: I love.'"*

Edward's manners and conduct caused her more real anxiety than anything else. Indeed, no other thoughtfulness could be called anxiety compared to this. His faults, she could not but perceive, were strengthening with his strength, and growing with his growth. She could not help wondering whence he obtained the money to pay for his dress, which she thought was of a very expensive kind. She heard him also incidentally allude to "runs up to town," of which, at the time, neither she nor her mother had been made aware. He seemed confused when she questioned him about these, although he tried to laugh it off; and asked her how she, a country girl, cooped up among one set of people, could have any idea of the life it was necessary for a man to lead who "had any hope of getting on in the world." He must have acquaintances and connections, and see something of life, and make an appearance. She was silenced, but not satisfied. Nor was she at ease with regard to his health. He looked ill, and worn; and, when he was not rattling and laughing, his face fell into a shape of anxiety and uneasiness, which was new to her in it. He reminded her painfully of an old German engraving she had seen in Mrs. Buxton's portfolio, called, "Pleasure digging a Grave;" Pleasure being represented by a ghastly figure of a young man, eagerly industrious over his dismal work.

A few days after he went away, Nancy came to her in her bed-room.

"Miss Maggie," said she, "may I just speak a word?" But when the permission was given, she hesitated.

"It's none of my business, to be sure," said she at last: "only, you see, I've lived with your mother ever since she was married; and I care a deal for both you and Master Edward. And I think he drains Missus of her money; and it makes me not easy in my mind. You did not know of it, but he had his father's old watch when he was over last time but one; I thought he was of an age to have a watch, and that it was all natural. But, I reckon he's sold it, and got that gimcrack one instead. That's perhaps natural too. Young folks like young fashions. But, this time, I think he has taken away your mother's watch; at least, I've never seen it since he went. And this morning she spoke to me about my wages. I'm sure I've never asked for them, nor troubled her; but I'll own it's now near on to twelve months since she paid me; and she was as regular as clock-work till then. Now, Miss Maggie don't look so sorry, or I shall wish I had never spoken. Poor Missus seemed sadly put about, and said something as I did not try to hear; for I was so vexed she should think I needed apologies, and them sort of things. I'd rather live with you without wages than have her look so shame-faced as she did this morning. I don't want a bit for money, my dear; I've a deal in the Bank. But I'm afeard Master Edward is spending too much, and pinching Missus."

Maggie was very sorry indeed. Her mother had never told her anything of all this, so it was evidently a painful subject to her; and Maggie determined (after lying awake half the night) that she would write to Edward, and remonstrate with him; and that in every personal and household expense, she would be, more than ever, rigidly economical.

The full, free, natural intercourse between her lover and herself, could not fail to be checked by Mr. Buxton's aversion to the engagement. Frank came over for some time in the early autumn. He had left Cambridge, and intended to enter himself at the Temple as soon as the vacation was ended. He had not been very long at home before Maggie was made aware, partly through Erminia, who had no notion of discreet silence on any point, and partly by her own observation, of the increasing estrangement between father and son. Mr. Buxton was reserved with Frank for the first time in his life; and Frank was depressed and annoyed at his father's obstinate repetition of the same sentence, in answer to all his arguments in favor of his engagement—arguments which were overwhelming to himself and which it required an effort of patience on his part to go over and recapitulate, so obvious was the conclusion; and then to have the same answer forever, the same words even:

"Frank! it's no use talking. I don't approve of the engagement; and never shall."

He would snatch up his hat, and hurry off to Maggie to be soothed. His father knew where he was gone without being told; and was jealous of her influence over the son who had long been his first and paramount object in life.

He needed not have been jealous. However angry and indignant Frank was when he went up to the moorland cottage,

Maggie almost persuaded him, before half an hour had elapsed, that his father was but unreasonable from his extreme affection. Still she saw that such frequent differences would weaken the bond between father and son; and, accordingly, she urged Frank to accept an invitation into Scotland.

"You told me," said she, "that Mr. Buxton will have it, it is but a boy's attachment; and that when you have seen other people, you will change your mind; now do try how far you can stand the effects of absence." She said it playfully, but he was in a humor to be vexed.

"What nonsense, Maggie! You don't care for all this delay yourself; and you take up my father's bad reasons as if you believed them."

"I don't believe them; but still they may be true."

"How should you like it, Maggie, if I urged you to go about and see something of society, and try if you could not find some one you liked better? It is more probable in your case than in mine; for you have never been from home, and I have been half over Europe."

"You are very much afraid, are not you, Frank?" said she, her face bright with blushes, and her gray eyes smiling up at him. "I have a great idea that if I could see that Harry Bish that Edward is always talking about, I should be charmed. He must wear such beautiful waistcoats! Don't you think I had better see him before our engagement is quite, quite final?"

But Frank would not smile. In fact, like all angry persons, he found fresh matter for offence in every sentence. She did not consider the engagement as quite final: thus he chose to understand her playful speech. He would not answer. She spoke again:

"Dear Frank, you are not angry with me, are you? It is nonsense to think that we are to go about the world, picking and choosing men and women as if they were fruit and we were to gather the best; as if there was not something in our own hearts which, if we listen to it conscientiously, will tell us at once when we have met the one of all others. There now, am I sensible? I suppose I am, for your grim features are relaxing into a smile. That's right. But now listen to this. I think your father would come round sooner, if he were not irritated every day by the knowledge of your visits to me. If you went away, he would know that we should write to each other yet he would forget the exact time when; but now he knows as well as I do where you are when you are up here; and I fancy, from what Erminia says, it makes him angry the whole time you are away."

Frank was silent. At last he said: "It is rather provoking to be obliged to acknowledge that there is some truth in what you say. But even if I would, I am not sure that I could go. My father does not speak to me about his affairs, as he used to do; so I was rather surprised yesterday to hear him say to Erminia (though I'm sure he meant the information for me), that he had engaged an agent."

"Then there will be the less occasion for you to be at home. He won't want your help in his accounts."

"I've given him little enough of that. I have long wanted him to have somebody to look after his affairs. They are very complicated and he is very careless. But I believe my signature will be wanted for some new leases; at least he told me so."

"That need not take you long," said Maggie.

"Not the mere signing. But I want to know something more about the property, and the proposed tenants. I believe this Mr. Henry that my father has engaged, is a very hard sort of man. He is what is called scrupulously honest and honorable; but I fear a little too much inclined to drive hard bargains for his client. Now I want to be convinced to the contrary, if I can, before I leave my father in his hands. So you cruel judge, you won't transport me yet, will you?"

"No" said Maggie, overjoyed at her own decision, and blushing her delight that her reason was convinced it was right for Frank to stay a little longer.

The next day's post brought her a letter from Edward. There was not a word in it about her inquiry or remonstrance; it might never have been written, or never received; but a few hurried anxious lines, asking her to write by return of post, and say if it was really true that Mr. Buxton had engaged an agent. "It's a confounded shabby trick if he has, after what he said to me long ago. I cannot tell you how much I depend on your complying with my request. Once more, *write directly*. If Nancy cannot take the letter to the post, run down to Combehurst with it yourself. I must have an answer to-morrow, and every particular as to who—when to be appointed, &c. But I can't believe the report to be true."

Maggie asked Frank if she might name what he had told her the day before to her brother. He said:

"Oh, yes, certainly, if he cares to know. Of course, you will not say anything about my own opinion of Mr. Henry. He is coming to-morrow, and I shall be able to judge how far I am right."

Chapter VII.

The next day Mr. Henry came. He was a quiet, stern-looking man, of considerable intelligence and refinement, and so much taste for music as to charm Erminia, who had rather dreaded his visit. But all the amenities of life were put aside when he entered Mr. Buxton's sanctum—his "office," as he called the room where he received his tenants and business people. Frank thought Mr. Henry was scarce commonly civil in the open evidence of his surprise and contempt for the habits, of which the disorderly books and ledgers were but too visible signs. Mr. Buxton himself felt more like a school-boy, bringing up an imperfect lesson, than he had ever done since he was thirteen.

"The only wonder, my good sir, is that you have any property left; that you have not been cheated out of every farthing."

"I'll answer for it," said Mr. Buxton, in reply, "that you'll not find any cheating has been going on. They dared not, sir; they know I should make an example of the first rogue I found out."

Mr. Henry lifted up his eyebrows, but did not speak.

"Besides, sir, most of these men have lived for generations under the Buxtons. I'd give you my life, they would not cheat me."

Mr. Henry coldly said:

"I imagine a close examination of these books by some accountant will be the best proof of the honesty of these said tenants. If you will allow me, I will write to a clever fellow I know, and desire him to come down and try and regulate this mass of papers."

"Anything—anything you like," said Mr. Buxton, only too glad to escape from the lawyer's cold, contemptuous way of treating the subject.

The accountant came; and he and Mr. Henry were deeply engaged in the office for several days. Mr. Buxton was bewildered by the questions they asked him. Mr. Henry examined him in the worrying way in which an unwilling witness is made to give evidence. Many a time and oft did he heartily wish he had gone on in the old course to the end of his life, instead of putting himself into an agent's hands; but he comforted himself by thinking that, at any rate, they would be convinced he had never allowed himself to be cheated or imposed upon, although he did not make any parade of exactitude.

What was his dismay when, one morning, Mr. Henry sent to request his presence, and, with a cold, clear voice, read aloud an admirably drawn up statement, informing the poor landlord of the defalcations, nay more, the impositions of those whom he had trusted. If he had been alone, he would have burst into tears, to find how his confidence had been abused. But as it was, he became passionately angry.

"I'll prosecute them, sir. Not a man shall escape. I'll make them pay back every farthing, I will. And damages, too. Crayston, did you say, sir? Was that one of the names? Why, that is the very Crayston who was bailiff under my father for years. The scoundrel! And I set him up in my best farm when he married. And he's been swindling me, has he?"

Mr. Henry ran over the items of the account—"421*l*, 13*s*. 4-3/4*d*. Part of this I fear we cannot recover—"

He was going on, but Mr. Buxton broke in: "But I will recover it. I'll have every farthing of it. I'll go to law with the viper. I don't care for money, but I hate ingratitude."

"If you like, I will take counsel's opinion on the case," said Mr. Henry, coolly.

"Take anything you please, sir. Why this Crayston was the first man that set me on a horse—and to think of his cheating me!"

A few days after this conversation, Frank came on his usual visit to Maggie.

"Can you come up to the thorn-tree, dearest?" said he. "It is a lovely day, and I want the solace of a quiet hour's talk with you."

So they went, and sat in silence some time, looking at the calm and still blue air about the summits of the hills, where never tumult of the world came to disturb the peace, and the quiet of whose heights was never broken by the loud passionate cries of men.

"I am glad you like my thorn-tree," said Maggie.

"I like the view from it. The thought of the solitude which must be among the hollows of those hills pleases me particularly to-day. Oh, Maggie! it is one of the times when I get depressed about men and the world. We have had such sorrow, and such revelations, and remorse, and passion at home to-day.

Crayston (my father's old tenant) has come over. It seems—I am afraid there is no doubt of it—he has been peculating to a large amount. My father has been too careless, and has placed his dependents in great temptation; and Crayston—he is an old man, with a large extravagant family—has yielded. He has been served with notice of my father's intention to prosecute him; and came over to confess all, and ask for forgiveness, and time to pay back what he could. A month ago, my father would have listened to him, I think; but now, he is stung by Mr. Henry's sayings, and gave way to a furious passion. It has been a most distressing morning. The worst side of everybody seems to have come out. Even Crayston, with all his penitence and appearance of candor, had to be questioned closely by Mr. Henry before he would tell the whole truth. Good God! that money should have such power to corrupt men. It was all for money, and money's worth, that this degradation has taken place. As for Mr. Henry, to save his client money, and to protect money, he does not care—he does not even perceive—how he induces deterioration of character. He has been encouraging my father in measures which I cannot call anything but vindictive. Crayston is to be made an example of, they say. As if my father had not half the sin on his own head! As if he had rightly discharged his duties as a rich man! Money was as dross to him; but he ought to have remembered how it might be as life itself to many, and be craved after, and coveted, till the black longing got the better of principle, as it has done with this poor Crayston. They say the man was once so truthful, and now his self-respect is gone; and he has evidently lost the very nature of truth. I dread riches. I dread the responsibility of them. At any rate, I wish I had begun life as a poor boy, and worked my way up to competence. Then I could understand and remember the temptations of poverty. I am afraid of my own heart becoming hardened as my father's is.

You have no notion of his passionate severity to-day, Maggie! It was quite a new thing even to me!"

"It will only be for a short time," said she. "He must be much grieved about this man."

"If I thought I could ever grow as hard and different to the abject entreaties of a criminal as my father has been this morning—one whom he has helped to make, too—I would go off to Australia at once. Indeed, Maggie, I think it would be the best thing we could do. My heart aches about the mysterious corruptions and evils of an old state of society such as we have in England.—What do you say Maggie? Would you go?"

She was silent—thinking.

"I would go with you directly, if it were right," said she, at last. "But would it be? I think it would be rather cowardly. I feel what you say; but don't you think it would be braver to stay, and endure much depression and anxiety of mind, for the sake of the good those always can do who see evils clearly. I am speaking all this time as if neither you nor I had any home duties, but were free to do as me liked."

"What can you or I do? We are less than drops in the ocean, as far as our influence can go to model a nation?"

"As for that," said Maggie, laughing, "I can't remodel Nancy's old-fashioned ways; so I've never yet planned how to remodel a nation."

"Then what did you mean by the good those always can do who see evils clearly? The evils I see are those of a nation whose god is money."

"That is just because you have come away from a distressing scene. To-morrow you will hear or read of some heroic action meeting with a nation's sympathy, and you will rejoice and be proud of your country."

"Still I shall see the evils of her complex state of society keenly; and where is the good I can do?"

"Oh! I can't tell in a minute. But cannot you bravely face these evils, and learn their nature and causes; and then has God given you no powers to apply to the discovery of their remedy? Dear Frank, think! It may be very little you can do—and you may never see the effect of it, any more than the widow saw the world-wide effect of her mite. Then if all the good and thoughtful men run away from us to some new country, what are we to do with our poor dear Old England?"

"Oh, you must run away with the good, thoughtful men—(I mean to consider that as a compliment to myself, Maggie!) Will you let me wish I had been born poor, if I am to stay in England? I should not then be liable to this fault into which I see the rich men fall, of forgetting the trials of the poor."

"I am not sure whether, if you had been poor, you might not have fallen into an exactly parallel fault, and forgotten the trials of the rich. It is so difficult to understand the errors into which their position makes all men liable to fall. Do you remember a story in 'Evenings at Home,' called the Transmigrations of Indra? Well! when I was a child, I used to wish I might be transmigrated (is that the right word?) into an American slave-owner for a little while, just that I might understand how he must suffer, and be sorely puzzled, and pray and long to be freed from his odious wealth, till at last he grew hardened to its nature;—and since then, I have wished to be the Emperor of Russia, for the same reason. Ah! you may laugh; but that is only because I have not explained myself properly."

"I was only smiling to think how ambitious any one might suppose you were who did not know you."

"I don't see any ambition in it—I don't think of the station—I only want sorely to see the 'What's resisted' of Burns, in order that I may have more charity for those who seem to me to have been the cause of such infinite woe and misery."

> *"'What's done we partly may compute;*
> *But know not what's resisted,'"*

repeated Frank musingly. After some time he began again:

"But, Maggie, I don't give up this wish of mine to go to Australia—Canada, if you like it better—anywhere where there is a newer and purer state of society."

"The great objection seems to be your duty, as an only child, to your father. It is different to the case of one out of a large family."

"I wish I were one in twenty, then I might marry where I liked to-morrow."

"It would take two people's consent to such a rapid measure," said Maggie, laughing. "But now I am going to wish a wish, which it won't require a fairy godmother to gratify. Look, Frank, do you see in the middle of that dark brown purple streak of moor a yellow gleam of light? It is a pond, I think, that at this time of the year catches a slanting beam of the sun. It cannot be very far off. I have wished to go to it every autumn. Will you go with me now? We shall have time before tea."

Frank's dissatisfaction with the stern measures that, urged on by Mr. Henry, his father took against all who had imposed upon his carelessness as a landlord, increased rather than diminished. He spoke warmly to him on the subject, but without avail. He remonstrated with Mr. Henry, and told him how he felt that, had his father controlled his careless nature, and been an exact, vigilant landlord, these tenantry would never have had the great temptation to do him wrong; and that therefore he considered some allowance should be made for them, and some opportunity given them to redeem their characters, which would be blasted and hardened for ever by the publicity of a law-suit. But Mr. Henry only raised his eyebrows and made answer:

"I like to see these notions in a young man, sir. I had them myself at your age. I believe I had great ideas then, on the subject of temptation and the force of circumstances; and was as Quixotic as any one about reforming rogues. But my experience has convinced me that roguery is innate. Nothing but outward force can control it, and keep it within bounds. The terrors of the law must be that outward force. I admire your kindness of heart; and in three-and-twenty we do not look for the wisdom and experience of forty or fifty."

Frank was indignant at being set aside as an unripe youth. He disapproved so strongly of all these measures, and of so much that was now going on at home under Mr. Henry's influence that he determined to pay his long promised visit to Scotland; and Maggie, sad at heart to see how he was suffering, encouraged him in his determination.

Chapter VIII.

After he was gone, there came a November of the most dreary and characteristic kind. There was incessant rain, and closing-in mists, without a gleam of sunshine to light up the drops of water, and make the wet stems and branches of the trees glisten. Every color seemed dimmed and darkened; and the crisp autumnal glory of leaves fell soddened to the ground. The latest flowers rotted away without ever coming to their bloom; and it looked as if the heavy monotonous sky had drawn closer and closer, and shut in the little moorland cottage as with a shroud. In doors, things were no more cheerful. Maggie saw that her mother was depressed, and she thought that Edward's extravagance must be the occasion. Oftentimes she wondered how far she might speak on the subject; and once or twice she drew near it in conversation; but her mother winced away, and Maggie could not as yet see any decided good to be gained from encountering such pain. To herself it would have been a relief to have known the truth—the worst, as far as her mother knew it; but she was not in the habit of thinking of herself. She only tried, by long tender attention, to cheer and comfort her mother; and she and Nancy strove in every way to reduce the household expenditure, for there was little ready money to meet it. Maggie wrote regularly to Edward; but since the note inquiring about the agency, she had never heard from him. Whether her mother received letters she did not know; but at any rate she did not express anxiety, though her looks and manner betrayed that she was ill at ease. It was almost a relief to Maggie when some change was given to her thoughts by Nancy's becoming ill. The damp gloomy weather brought on some kind of rheumatic attack, which obliged the old servant to keep her bed. Formerly, in such an emergency, they would have engaged some cottager's wife to come and do the house-work; but now it seemed tacitly understood that they could not afford it. Even when Nancy grew worse, and required attendance in the night, Maggie still persisted in her daily occupations. She was wise enough to rest when and how she could; and, with a little forethought, she hoped to be able to go through this weary time without any bad effect. One morning (it was on the second of December; and even the change of name in the month, although it brought no change of circumstances or weather, was a relief—December brought glad tidings even in its very name), one morning, dim and dreary, Maggie had looked at the clock on leaving Nancy's room, and finding it was not yet half-past five, and knowing that her mother and Nancy were both asleep, she determined to lie down and rest for an hour before getting up to light the fires. She did not mean to go to sleep; but she was tired out and fell into a sound slumber. When she awoke it was with a start. It was still dark; but she had a clear idea of being wakened by some distinct, rattling noise. There it was once more—against the window, like a shower of shot. She went to the lattice, and opened it to look out. She had that strange consciousness, not to be described, of the near neighborhood of some human creature, although she neither saw nor heard any one for the first instant. Then Edward spoke in a hoarse whisper, right below the window, standing on the flower-beds.

"Maggie! Maggie! Come down and let me in. For your life, don't make any noise. No one must know."

Maggie turned sick. Something was wrong, evidently; and she was weak and weary. However, she stole down the old creaking stairs, and undid the heavy bolt, and let her brother in. She felt that his dress was quite wet, and she led him, with cautious steps, into the kitchen, and shut the door, and stirred the fire, before she spoke. He sank into a chair, as if worn out with fatigue. She stood, expecting some explanation. But when she saw he could not speak, she hastened to make him a cup of tea; and, stooping down, took off his wet boots, and helped him off with his coat, and brought her own plaid to wrap round him. All this time her heart sunk lower and lower. He allowed her to do what she liked, as if he were an automaton; his head and his arms hung loosely down, and his eyes were fixed, in a glaring way, on the fire. When she brought him some tea, he spoke for the first time; she could not hear what he said till he repeated it, so husky was his voice.

"Have you no brandy?"

She had the key of the little wine-cellar, and fetched up some. But as she took a tea-spoon to measure if out, he tremblingly clutched at the bottle, and shook down a quantity into the empty tea-cup, and drank it off at one gulp. He fell back again in his chair; but in a few minutes he roused himself, and seemed stronger.

"Edward, dear Edward, what is the matter?" said Maggie, at last; for he got up, and was staggering toward the outer door, as if he were going once more into the rain, and dismal morning-twilight.

He looked at her fiercely as she laid her hand on his arm.

"Confound you! Don't touch me. I'll not be kept here, to be caught and hung!"

For an instant she thought he was mad.

"Caught and hung!" she echoed. "My poor Edward! what do you mean?"

He sat down suddenly on a chair, close by him, and covered his face with his hands. When he spoke, his voice was feeble and imploring.

"The police are after me, Maggie! What must I do? Oh! can you hide me? Can you save me?"

He looked wild, like a hunted creature. Maggie stood aghast. He went on:

"My mother!—Nancy! Where are they? I was wet through and starving, and I came here. Don't let them take me, Maggie, till I'm stronger, and can give battle."

"Oh! Edward! Edward! What are you saying?" said Maggie, sitting down on the dresser, in absolute, bewildered despair. "What have you done?"

"I hardly know. I'm in a horrid dream. I see you think I'm mad. I wish I were. Won't Nancy come down soon? You must hide me."

"Poor Nancy is ill in bed!" said Maggie.

"Thank God," said he. "There's one less. But my mother will be up soon, will she not?"

"Not yet," replied Maggie. "Edward, dear, do try and tell me what you have done. Why should the police be after you?"

"Why, Maggie," said he with a kind of forced, unnatural laugh, "they say I've forged."

"And have you?" asked Maggie, in a still, low tone of quiet agony.

He did not answer for some time, but sat, looking on the floor with unwinking eyes. At last he said, as if speaking to himself:

"If I have, it's no more than others have done before, and never been found out. I was but borrowing money. I meant to repay it. If I had asked Mr. Buxton, he would have lent it me."

"Mr. Buxton!" said Maggie.

"Yes!" answered he, looking sharply and suddenly up at her. "Your future father-in-law. My father's old friend. It is he that is hunting me to death! No need to look so white and horror-struck, Maggie! It's the way of the world, as I might have known, if I had not been a blind fool."

"Mr. Buxton!" she whispered, faintly.

"Oh, Maggie!" said he, suddenly throwing himself at her feet, "save me! You can do it. Write to Frank, and make him induce his father to let me off. I came to see you, my sweet, merciful sister! I knew you would save me. Good God! What noise is that? There are steps in the yard!"

And before she could speak, he had rushed into the little china closet, which opened out of the parlor, and crouched down in the darkness. It was only the man who brought their morning's supply of milk from a neighboring farm. But when Maggie opened the kitchen door, she saw how the cold, pale light of a winter's day had filled the air.

"You're late with your shutters to-day, miss," said the man. "I hope Nancy has not been giving you all a bad night. Says I to Thomas, who came with me to the gate, 'It's many a year since I saw them parlor shutters barred up at half-past eight.'"

Maggie went, as soon as he was gone, and opened all the low windows, in order that they might look as usual. She wondered at her own outward composure, while she felt so dead and sick at heart. Her mother would soon get up; must she be told? Edward spoke to her now and then from his hiding-place. He dared not go back into the kitchen, into which the few neighbors they had were apt to come, on their morning's way to Combehurst, to ask if they could do any errands there for Mrs. Browne or Nancy. Perhaps a quarter of an hour or so had elapsed since the first alarm, when, as Maggie was trying to light the parlor fire, in order that the doctor, when he came, might find all as usual, she heard the click of the garden gate, and a man's step coming along the walk. She ran up stairs to wash away the traces of the tears which had been streaming down her face as she went about her work, before she opened the door. There, against the watery light of the rainy day without, stood Mr. Buxton. He hardly spoke to her, but pushed past her, and entered the parlor. He sat down, looking as if he did not know what he was doing. Maggie tried to keep down her shivering alarm. It was long since she had seen him; and the old idea of his kind, genial disposition, had been sadly disturbed by what she had heard from Frank, of his severe proceedings against his unworthy tenantry; and now, if he was setting the police in search of Edward, he was indeed to be dreaded; and with Edward so close at hand, within earshot! If the china fell! He would suspect nothing from that; it would only be her own terror. If her mother came down! But, with all these thoughts, she was very still, outwardly, as she sat waiting for him to speak.

"Have you heard from your brother lately?" asked he, looking up in an angry and disturbed manner. "But I'll answer for it he has not been writing home for some time. He could not, with the guilt he has had on his mind. I'll not believe in gratitude again. There perhaps was such a thing once; but now-a-days the more you do for a person, the surer they are to turn against you, and cheat you. Now, don't go white and pale. I know you're a good girl in the main; and I've been lying awake all night, and I've a deal to say to you. That scoundrel of a brother of yours!"

Maggie could not ask (as would have been natural, if she had been ignorant) what Edward had done. She knew too well. But Mr. Buxton was too full of his own thoughts and feelings to notice her much.

"Do you know he has been like the rest? Do you know he has been cheating me—forging my name? I don't know what besides. It's well for him that they've altered the laws, and he can't be hung for it" (a dead heavy weight was removed from Maggie's mind), "but Mr. Henry is going to transport him. It's worse than Crayston. Crayston only ploughed up the turf, and did not pay rent, and sold the timber, thinking I should never miss it. But your brother has gone and forged my name He had received all the purchase-money, while he only gave me half, and said the rest was to come afterward. And the ungrateful scoundrel has gone and given a forged receipt! You might have knocked me down with a straw when Mr. Henry told me about it all last night. 'Never talk to me of virtue and such humbug again,' I said, 'I'll never believe in them. Every one is for what he can get.' However, Mr. Henry wrote to the superintendent of police at Woodchester; and has gone over himself this morning to see after it. But to think of your father having such a son!"

"Oh my poor father!" sobbed out Maggie. "How glad I am you are dead before this disgrace came upon us!"

"You may well say disgrace. You're a good girl yourself, Maggie. I have always said that. How Edward has turned out as he has done, I cannot conceive. But now, Maggie, I've something to say to you." He moved uneasily about, as if he did not know how to begin. Maggie was standing leaning her head against the chimney-piece, longing for her visitor to go, dreading the next minute, and wishing to shrink into some dark corner of oblivion where she might forget all for a time, till she regained a small portion of the bodily strength that had been sorely tried of late. Mr. Buxton saw her white look of anguish, and read it in part, but not wholly. He was too intent on what he was going to say.

"I've been lying awake all night, thinking. You see the disgrace it is to you, though you are innocent; and I'm sure you can't think of involving Frank in it."

Maggie went to the little sofa, and, kneeling down by it, hid her face in the cushions. He did not go on, for he thought she was not listening to him. At last he said:

"Come now, be a sensible girl, and face it out. I've a plan to propose."

"I hear," said she, in a dull veiled voice.

"Why, you know how against this engagement I have always been. Frank is but three-and-twenty, and does not know his own mind, as I tell him. Besides, he might marry any one he chose."

"He has chosen me," murmured Maggie.

"Of course, of course. But you'll not think of keeping him to it, after what has passed. You would not have such a fine fellow as Frank pointed at as the brother-in-law of a forger, would you? It was far from what I wished for him before; but now! Why you're glad your father is dead, rather than he should have lived to see this day; and rightly too, I think. And you'll not go and disgrace Frank. From what Mr. Henry hears, Edward has been a discredit to you in many ways. Mr. Henry was at Woodchester yesterday, and he says if Edward has been fairly entered as an attorney, his name may be struck off the Rolls for many a thing he has done. Think of my Frank having his bright name tarnished by any connection with such a man! Mr. Henry says, even in a court of law what has come out about Edward would be excuse enough for a breach of promise of marriage."

Maggie lifted up her wan face; the pupils of her eyes were dilated, her lips were dead white. She looked straight at Mr. Buxton with indignant impatience:

"Mr. Henry! Mr. Henry! What has Mr. Henry to do with me?"

Mr. Buxton was staggered by the wild, imperious look, so new upon her mild, sweet face. But he was resolute for Frank's sake, and returned to the charge after a moment's pause.

"Mr. Henry is a good friend of mine, who has my interest at heart. He has known what a subject of regret your engagement has been to me; though really my repugnance to it was without cause formerly, compared to what it is now. Now be reasonable, my dear. I'm willing to do something for you if you will do something for me. You must see what a stop this sad affair has put to any thoughts between you and Frank. And you must see what cause I have to wish to punish Edward for his ungrateful behavior, to say nothing of the forgery. Well now! I don't know what Mr. Henry will say to me, but I have thought of this. If you'll write a letter to Frank, just saying distinctly that, for reasons which must for ever remain a secret..."

"Remain a secret from Frank?" said Maggie, again lifting up her head. "Why?"

"Why? my dear! You startle me with that manner of yours—just let me finish out my sentence. If you'll say that, for reasons which must forever remain a secret, you decidedly and unchangeably give up all connection, all engagement with him (which, in fact, Edward's conduct has as good as put an end to), I'll go over to Woodchester and tell Mr. Henry and the police that they need not make further search after Edward, for that I won't appear against him. You can save your brother; and you'll do yourself no harm by writing this letter, for of course you see your engagement is broken off. For you never would wish to disgrace Frank."

He paused, anxiously awaiting her reply. She did not speak.

"I'm sure, if I appear against him, he is as good as transported," he put in, after a while.

Just at this time there was a little sound of displaced china in the closet. Mr. Buxton did not attend to it, but Maggie heard it. She got up, and stood quite calm before Mr. Buxton.

"You must go," said she. "I know you; and I know you are not aware of the cruel way in which you have spoken to me, while asking me to give up the very hope and marrow of my life"—she could not go on for a moment; she was choked up with anguish.

"It was the truth, Maggie," said he, somewhat abashed.

"It was the truth that made the cruelty of it. But you did not mean to speak cruelly to me, I know. Only it is hard all at once to be called upon to face the shame and blasted character of one who was once an innocent child at the same father's knee."

"I may have spoken too plainly," said Mr. Buxton, "but it was necessary to set the plain truth before you, for my son's sake. You will write the letter I ask?"

Her look was wandering and uncertain. Her attention was distracted by sounds which to him had no meaning; and her judgment she felt was wavering and disturbed.

"I cannot tell. Give me time to think; you will do that, I'm sure. Go now, and leave me alone. If it is right, God will give me strength to do it, and perhaps He will comfort me in my desolation. But I do not know—I cannot tell. I must have time to think. Go now, if you please, sir," said she, imploringly.

"I am sure you will see it is a right thing I ask of you," he persisted.

"Go now," she repeated.

"Very well. In two hours, I will come back again; for your sake, time is precious. Even while we speak he may be arrested. At eleven, I will come back."

He went away, leaving her sick and dizzy with the effort to be calm and collected enough to think. She had forgotten for the moment how near Edward was; and started when she saw the closet-door open, and his face put out.

"Is he gone? I thought he never would go. What a time you kept him, Maggie! I was so afraid, once, you might sit down to write the letter in this room; and then I knew he would stop and worry you with interruptions and advice, so that it would never be ended; and my back was almost broken. But you sent him off famously. Why, Maggie! Maggie!—you're not going to faint, surely!"

His sudden burst out of a whisper into a loud exclamation of surprise, made her rally; but she could not stand. She tried to smile, for he really looked frightened.

"I have been sitting up for many nights—and now this sorrow!" Her smile died away into a wailing, feeble cry.

"Well, well! it's over now, you see. I was frightened enough myself this morning, I own; and then you were brave and kind. But I knew you could save me, all along."

At this moment the door opened, and Mrs. Browne came in.

"Why, Edward, dear! who would have thought of seeing you! This is good of you; what a pleasant surprise! I often said, you might come over for a day from Woodchester. What's the matter, Maggie, you look so fagged? She's losing all her beauty, is not she, Edward? Where's breakfast? I thought I should find all ready. What's the matter? Why don't you speak?" said she, growing anxious at their silence. Maggie left the explanation to Edward.

"Mother," said he, "I've been rather a naughty boy, and got into some trouble; but Maggie is going to help me out of it, like a good sister."

"What is it?" said Mrs. Browne, looking bewildered and uneasy.

"Oh—I took a little liberty with our friend Mr. Buxton's name; and wrote it down to a receipt—that was all."

Mrs. Browne's face showed that the light came but slowly into her mind.

"But that's forgery—is not it?" asked she at length, in terror.

"People call it so," said Edward; "I call it borrowing from an old friend, who was always willing to lend."

"Does he know?—is he angry?" asked Mrs. Browne.

"Yes, he knows; and he blusters a deal. He was working himself up grandly at first. Maggie! I was getting rarely frightened, I can tell you."

"Has he been here?" said Mrs. Browne, in bewildered fright.

"Oh, yes! he and Maggie have been having a long talk, while I was hid in the china-closet. I would not go over that half-hour again for any money. However, he and Maggie came to terms, at last."

"No, Edward, we did not!" said Maggie, in a low quivering voice.

"Very nearly. She's to give up her engagement, and then he will let me off."

"Do you mean that Maggie is to give up her engagement to Mr. Frank Buxton?" asked his mother.

"Yes. It would never have come to anything, one might see that. Old Buxton would have held out against it till doomsday. And, sooner or later, Frank would have grown weary. If Maggie had had any spirit, she might have worked him up to marry her before now; and then I should have been spared even this fright, for they would never have set the police after Mrs. Frank Buxton's brother."

"Why, dearest, Edward, the police are not after you, are they?" said Mrs. Browne, for the first time alive to the urgency of the case.

"I believe they are though," said Edward. "But after what Mr. Buxton promised this morning, it does not signify."

"He did not promise anything," said Maggie.

Edward turned sharply to her, and looked at her. Then he went and took hold of her wrists with no gentle grasp, and spoke to her through his set teeth.

"What do you mean, Maggie?—what do you mean?" (giving her a little shake.) "Do you mean that you'll stick to your lover through thick and thin, and leave your brother to be transported? Speak, can't you?"

She looked up at him, and tried to speak, but no words came out of her dry throat. At last she made a strong effort.

"You must give me time to think. I will do what is right, by God's help."

"As if it was not right—and such can't—to save your brother," said he, throwing her hands away in a passionate manner.

"I must be alone," said Maggie, rising, and trying to stand steadily in the reeling room. She heard her mother and Edward speaking, but their words gave her no meaning, and she went out. She was leaving the house by the kitchen-door, when she remembered Nancy, left alone and helpless all through this long morning; and, ill as she could endure detention from the solitude she longed to seek, she patiently fulfilled her small duties, and sought out some breakfast for the poor old woman.

When she carried it up stairs, Nancy said:

"There's something up. You've trouble in your sweet face, my darling. Never mind telling me—only don't sob so. I'll pray for you, bairn: and God will help you."

"Thank you, Nancy. Do!" and she left the room.

Chapter IX.

When she opened the kitchen-door there was the same small, mizzling rain that had obscured the light for weeks, and now it seemed to obscure hope.

She clambered slowly (for indeed she was very feeble) up the Fell-Lane, and threw herself under the leafless thorn, every small branch and twig of which was loaded with rain-drops. She did not see the well-beloved and familiar landscape for her tears, and did not miss the hills in the distance that were hidden behind the rain-clouds, and sweeping showers.

Mrs. Browne and Edward sat over the fire. He told her his own story; making the temptation strong; the crime a mere trifling, venial error, which he had been led into, through his idea that he was to become Mr. Buxton's agent.

"But if it is only that," said Mrs. Browne, "surely Mr. Buxton will not think of going to law with you?"

"It's not merely going to law that he will think of, but trying and transporting me. That Henry he has got for his agent is as sharp as a needle, and as hard as a nether mill-stone. And the fellow has obtained such a hold over Mr. Buxton, that he dare but do what he tells him. I can't imagine how he had so much free-will left as to come with his proposal to Maggie; unless, indeed, Henry knows of it—or, what is most likely of all, has put him up to it. Between them they have given that poor fool Crayston a pretty dose of it; and I should have come yet worse off if it had not been for Maggie. Let me get clear this time, and I will keep to windward of the law for the future."

"If we sold the cottage we could repay it," said Mrs. Browne, meditating. "Maggie and I could live on very little. But you see this property is held in trust for you two."

"Nay, mother; you must not talk of repaying it. Depend upon it he will be so glad to have Frank free from his engagement, that he won't think of asking for the money. And if Mr. Henry says anything about it, we can tell him it's not half the damages they would have had to have given Maggie, if Frank had been extricated in any other way. I wish she would come back; I would prime her a little as to what to say. Keep a look out, mother, lest Mr. Buxton returns and find me here."

"I wish Maggie would come in too," said Mrs. Browne. "I'm afraid she'll catch cold this damp day, and then I shall have two to nurse. You think she'll give it up, don't you, Edward? If she does not I'm afraid of harm coming to you. Had you not better keep out of the way?"

"It's fine talking. Where am I to go out of sight of the police this wet day: without a shilling in the world too? If you'll give me some money I'll be off fast enough, and make assurance doubly sure. I'm not much afraid of Maggie. She's a little yea-nay thing, and I can always bend her round to what we want. She had better take care, too," said he, with a desperate look on his face, "for by G—— I'll make her give up all thoughts of Frank, rather than be taken and tried. Why! it's my chance for all my life; and do you think I'll have it frustrated for a girl's whim?"

"I think it's rather hard upon her too," pleaded his mother. "She's very fond of him; and it would have been such a good match for her."

"Pooh! she's not nineteen yet, and has plenty of time before her to pick up somebody else; while, don't you see, if I'm caught and transported, I'm done for life. Besides I've a notion Frank had already begun to be tired of the affair; it would have been broken off in a month or two, without her gaining anything by it."

"Well, if you think so," replied Mrs. Browne. "But I'm sorry for her. I always told her she was foolish to think so much about him: but I know she'll fret a deal if it's given up."

"Oh! she'll soon comfort herself with thinking that she has saved me. I wish she'd come. It must be near eleven. I do wish she would come. Hark! is not that the kitchen-door?" said he, turning white, and betaking himself once more to the china-closet. He held it ajar till he heard Maggie stepping softly and slowly across the floor. She opened the parlor-door; and stood looking in, with the strange imperceptive gaze of a sleep-walker. Then she roused herself and saw that he was not there; so she came in a step or two, and sat down in her dripping cloak on a chair near the door.

Edward returned, bold now there was no danger.

"Maggie!" said he, "what have you fixed to say to Mr. Burton?"

She sighed deeply; and then lifted up her large innocent eyes to his face.

"I cannot give up Frank," said she, in a low, quiet voice.

Mrs. Browne threw up her hands and exclaimed in terror:

"Oh Edward, Edward! go away—I will give you all the plate I have; you can sell it—my darling, go!"

"Not till I have brought Maggie to reason," said he, in a manner as quiet as her own, but with a subdued ferocity in it, which she saw, but which did not intimidate her.

He went up to her, and spoke below his breath.

"Maggie, we were children together—we two—brother and sister of one blood! Do you give me up to be put in prison— in the hulks—among the basest of criminals—I don't know where—all for the sake of your own selfish happiness?"

She trembled very much; but did not speak or cry, or make any noise.

"You were always selfish. You always thought of yourself. But this time I did think you would have shown how different you could be. But it's self—self—paramount above all."

"Oh Maggie! how can you be so hard-hearted and selfish?" echoed Mrs. Browne, crying and sobbing.

"Mother!" said Maggie, "I know that I think too often and too much of myself. But this time I thought only of Frank. He loves me; it would break his heart if I wrote as Mr. Buxton wishes, cutting our lives asunder, and giving no reason for it."

"He loves you so!" said Edward, tauntingly. "A man's love break his heart! You've got some pretty notions! Who told you that he loved you so desperately? How do you know it?"

"Because I love him so," said she, in a quiet, earnest voice. "I do not know of any other reason; but that is quite sufficient to me. I believe him when he says he loves me; and I have no right to cause him the infinite—the terrible pain, which my own heart tells me he would feel, if I did what Mr. Buxton wishes me."

Her manner was so simple and utterly truthful, that it was as quiet and fearless as a child's; her brother's fierce looks of anger had no power over her; and his blustering died away before her into something of the frightened cowardliness he had shown in the morning. But Mrs. Browne came up to Maggie; and took her hand between both of hers, which were trembling. "Maggie, you can save Edward. I know I have not loved you as I should have done; but I will love and comfort you forever, if you will but write as Mr. Buxton says. Think! Perhaps Mr. Frank may not take you at your word, but may come over and see you, and all may be right, and yet Edward may be saved. It is only writing this letter; you need not stick to it."

"No!" said Edward. "A signature, if you can prove compulsion, is not valid. We will all prove that you write this letter under compulsion; and if Frank loves you so desperately, he won't give you up without a trial to make you change your mind."

"No!" said Maggie, firmly. "If I write the letter I abide by it. I will not quibble with my conscience. Edward! I will not marry—I will go and live near you, and come to you whenever I may—and give up my life to you if you are sent to prison; my mother and I will go, if need be—I do not know yet what I can do, or cannot do, for you, but all I can I will; but this one thing I cannot."

"Then I'm off!" said Edward. "On your deathbed may you remember this hour, and how you denied your only brother's request. May you ask my forgiveness with your dying breath, and may I be there to deny it you."

"Wait a minute!" said Maggie, springing up, rapidly. "Edward, don't curse me with such terrible words till all is done. Mother, I implore you to keep him here. Hide him—do what you can to conceal him. I will have one more trial." She snatched up her bonnet, and was gone, before they had time to think or speak to arrest her.

On she flew along the Combehurst road. As she went, the tears fell like rain down her face, and she talked to herself.

"He should not have said so. No! he should not have said so. We were the only two." But still she pressed on, over the thick, wet, brown heather. She saw Mr. Buxton coming; and she went still quicker. The rain had cleared off, and a yellow watery gleam of sunshine was struggling out. She stopped or he would have passed her unheeded; little expecting to meet her there.

"I wanted to see you," said she, all at once resuming her composure, and almost assuming a dignified manner. "You must not go down to our house; we have sorrow enough there. Come under these fir-trees, and let me speak to you."

"I hope you have thought of what I said, and are willing to do what I asked you."

"No!" said she. "I have thought and thought. I did not think in a selfish spirit, though they say I did. I prayed first. I could not do that earnestly, and be selfish, I think. I cannot give up Frank. I know the disgrace; and if he, knowing all, thinks fit to give me up, I shall never say a word, but bow my head, and try and live out my appointed days quietly and cheerfully. But he is the judge, not you; nor have I any right to do what you ask me." She stopped, because the agitation took away her breath.

He began in a cold manner:—"I am very sorry. The law must take its course. I would have saved my son from the pain of all this knowledge, and that which he will of course feel in the necessity of giving up his engagement. I would have refused to appear against your brother, shamefully ungrateful as he has been. Now you cannot wonder that I act according to my agent's advice, and prosecute your brother as if he were a stranger."

He turned to go away. He was so cold and determined that for a moment Maggie was timid. But she then laid her hand on his arm.

"Mr. Buxton," said she, "you will not do what you threaten. I know you better. Think! My father was your old friend. That claim is, perhaps, done away with by Edward's conduct. But I do not believe you can forget it always. If you did fulfill the menace you uttered just now, there would come times as you grew older, and life grew fainter and fainter before you— quiet times of thought, when you remembered the days of your youth, and the friends you then had and knew;—you would recollect that one of them had left an only son, who had done wrong—who had sinned—sinned against you in his weakness— and you would think then—you could not help it—how you had forgotten mercy in justice—and, as justice required he should be treated as a felon, you threw him among felons—where every glimmering of goodness was darkened for ever. Edward is, after all, more weak than wicked;—but he will become wicked if you put him in prison, and have him transported. God is merciful— we cannot tell or think how merciful. Oh, sir, I am so sure you will be merciful, and give my brother—my poor sinning brother—a chance, that I will tell you all. I will throw myself upon your pity. Edward is even now at home—miserable and desperate;—my mother is too much stunned to understand all our wretchedness—for very wretched we are in our shame."

As she spoke the wind arose and shivered in the wiry leaves of the fir-trees, and there was a moaning sound as of some Ariel imprisoned in the thick branches that, tangled overhead, made a shelter for them. Either the noise or Mr. Buxton's fancy called up an echo to Maggie's voice—a pleading with her pleading—a sad tone of regret, distinct yet blending with her speech, and a falling, dying sound, as her voice died away in miserable suspense.

It might be that, formed as she was by Mrs. Buxton's care and love, her accents and words were such as that lady, now at rest from all sorrow, would have used;—somehow, at any rate, the thought flashed into Mr. Buxton's mind, that as Maggie spoke, his dead wife's voice was heard, imploring mercy in a clear, distinct tone, though faint, as if separated from him by an infinite distance of space. At least, this is the account Mr. Buxton would have given of the manner in which the idea of his wife became present to him, and what she would have wished him to do a powerful motive in his conduct. Words of hers, long ago spoken, and merciful, forgiving expressions made use of in former days to soften him in some angry mood, were clearly remembered while Maggie spoke; and their influence was perceptible in the change of his tone, and the wavering of his manner henceforward.

"And yet you will not save Frank from being involved in your disgrace," said he; but more as if weighing and deliberating on the case than he had ever spoken before.

"If Frank wishes it, I will quietly withdraw myself out of his sight forever;—I give you my promise, before God, to do so. I shall not utter one word of entreaty or complaint. I will try not to wonder or feel surprise;—I will bless him in every action of his future life—but think how different would be the disgrace he would voluntarily incur to my poor mother's shame, when she wakens up to know what her child has done! Her very torper about it now is more painful than words can tell."

"What could Edward do?" asked Mr. Buxton. "Mr. Henry won't hear of my passing over any frauds."

"Oh, you relent!" said Maggie, taking his hand, and pressing it. "What could he do? He could do the same, whatever it was, as you thought of his doing, if I had written that terrible letter."

"And you'll be willing to give it up, if Frank wishes, when he knows all?" asked Mr. Buxton.

She crossed her hands and drooped her head, but answered steadily.

"Whatever Frank wishes, when he knows all, I will gladly do. I will speak the truth. I do not believe that any shame surrounding me, and not in me, will alter Frank's love one title."

"We shall see," said Mr. Buxton. "But what I thought of Edward's doing, in case—Well never mind! (seeing how she shrunk back from all mention of the letter he had asked her to write,)—was to go to America, out of the way. Then Mr. Henry would think he had escaped, and need never be told of my coenivance. I think he would throw up the agency, if he were; and he's a very clever man. If Ned is in England, Mr. Henry will ferret him out. And, besides, this affair is so blown, I don't think he could return to his profession. What do you say to this, Maggie?"

"I will tell my mother. I must ask her. To me it seems most desirable. Only, I fear he is very ill; and it seems lonely; but never mind! We ought to be thankful to you forever. I cannot tell you how I hope and trust he will live to show you what your goodness has made him."

"But you must lose no time. If Mr. Henry traces him; I can't answer for myself. I shall have no good reason to give, as I should have had, if I could have told him that Frank and you were to be as strangers to each other. And even then I should have been afraid, he is such a determined fellow; but uncommonly clever. Stay!" said he, yielding to a sudden and inexplicable desire to see Edward, and discover if his criminality had in any way changed his outward appearance. "I'll go with you. I can hasten things. If Edward goes, he must be off, as soon as possible, to Liverpool, and leave no trace. The next packet sails the day after to-morrow. I noted it down from the *Times*."

Maggie and he sped along the road. He spoke his thoughts aloud:

"I wonder if he will be grateful to me for this. Not that I ever mean to look for gratitude again. I mean to try, not to care for anybody but Frank. 'Govern men by outward force,' says Mr. Henry. He is an uncommonly clever man, and he says, the longer he lives, the more he is convinced of the badness of men. He always looks for it now, even in those who are the best, apparently."

Maggie was too anxious to answer, or even to attend to him. At the top of the slope she asked him to wait while she ran down and told the result of her conversation with him. Her mother was alone, looking white and sick. She told her that Edward had gone into the hay-loft, above the old, disused shippon.

Maggie related the substance of her interview with Mr. Buxton, and his wish that Edward should go to America.

"To America!" said Mrs. Browne. "Why that's as far as Botany Bay. It's just like transporting him. I thought you'd done something for us, you looked so glad."

"Dearest mother, it *is* something. He is not to be subjected to imprisonment or trial. I must go and tell him, only I must beckon to Mr. Buxton first. But when he comes, do show him how thankful we are for his mercy to Edward."

Mrs. Browne's murmurings, whatever was their meaning, were lost upon Maggie. She ran through the court, and up the slope, with the lightness of a lawn; for though she was tired in body to an excess she had never been before in her life, the opening beam of hope in the dark sky made her spirit conquer her flesh for the time.

She did not stop to speak, but turned again as soon as she had signed to Mr. Buxton to follow her. She left the house-door open for his entrance, and passed out again through the kitchen into the space behind, which was partly an uninclosed yard, and partly rocky common. She ran across the little green to the shippon, and mounted the ladder into the dimly-lighted loft. Up in a dark corner Edward stood, with an old rake in his hand.

"I thought it was you, Maggie!" said he, heaving a deep breath of relief. "What have you done? Have you agreed to write the letter? You've done something for me, I see by your looks."

"Yes! I have told Mr. Buxton all. He is waiting for you in the parlor. Oh! I knew he could not be so hard!" She was out of breath.

"I don't understand you!" said he. "You've never been such a fool as to go and tell him where I am?"

"Yes, I have. I felt I might trust him. He has promised not to prosecute you. The worst is, he says you must go to America. But come down, Ned, and speak to him. You owe him thanks, and he wants to see you."

"I can't go through a scene. I'm not up to it. Besides, are you sure he is not entrapping me to the police? If I had a farthing of money I would not trust him, but be off to the moors."

"Oh, Edward! How do you think he would do anything so treacherous and mean? I beg you not to lose time in distrust. He says himself, if Mr. Henry comes before you are off, he does not know what will be the consequence. The packet sails for America in two days. It is sad for you to have to go. Perhaps even yet he may think of something better, though I don't know how we can ask or expect it."

"I don't want anything better," replied he, "than that I should have money enough to carry me to America. I'm in more scrapes than this (though none so bad) in England; and in America there's many an opening to fortune." He followed her down the steps while he spoke. Once in the yellow light of the watery day, she was struck by his ghastly look. Sharp lines of suspicion and cunning seemed to have been stamped upon his face, making it look older by many years than his age warranted. His jaunty evening dress, all weather-stained and dirty, added to his forlorn and disreputable appearance; but most of all— deepest of all—was the impression she received that he was not long for this world; and oh! how unfit for the next! Still, if time was given—if he were placed far away from temptation, she thought that her father's son might yet repent, and be saved. She took his hand, for he was hanging back as they came near the parlor-door, and led him in. She looked like some guardian angel, with her face that beamed out trust, and hope, and thankfulness. He, on the contrary, hung his head in angry, awkward shame; and half wished he had trusted to his own wits, and tried to evade the police, rather than have been forced into this interview.

His mother came to him; for she loved him all the more fondly, now he seemed degraded and friendless. She could not, or would not, comprehend the extent of his guilt; and had upbraided Mr. Buxton to the top of her bent for thinking of sending him away to America. There was a silence when he came in which was insupportable to him. He looked up with clouded eyes, that dared not meet Mr. Buxton's.

"I am here, sir, to learn what you wish me to do. Maggie says I am to go to America; if that is where you want to send me, I'm ready."

Mr. Buxton wished himself away as heartily as Edward. Mrs. Browne's upbraidings, just when he felt that he had done a kind action, and yielded, against his judgment, to Maggie's entreaties, had made him think himself very ill used. And now here was Edward speaking in a sullen, savage kind of way, instead of showing any gratitude. The idea of Mr. Henry's stern displeasure loomed in the background.

"Yes!" said he, "I'm glad to find you come into the idea of going to America. It's the only place for you. The sooner you can go, and the better."

"I can't go without money," said Edward, doggedly. "If I had had money, I need not have come here."

"Oh, Ned! would you have gone without seeing me?" said Mrs. Browne, bursting into tears. "Mr. Buxton, I cannot let him go to America. Look how ill he is. He'll die if you send him there."

"Mother, don't give way so," said Edward, kindly, taking her hand. "I'm not ill, at least not to signify. Mr. Buxton is right: America is the only place for me. To tell the truth, even if Mr. Buxton is good enough" (he said this as if unwilling to express any word of thankfulness) "not to prosecute me, there are others who may—and will. I'm safer out of the country. Give me money enough to get to Liverpool and pay my passage, and I'll be off this minute."

"You shall not," said Mrs. Browne, holding him tightly. "You told me this morning you were led into temptation, and went wrong because you had no comfortable home, nor any one to care for you, and make you happy. It will be worse in America. You'll get wrong again, and be away from all who can help you. Or you'll die all by yourself, in some backwood or other. Maggie! you might speak and help me—how can you stand so still, and let him go to America without a word!"

Maggie looked up bright and steadfast, as if she saw something beyond the material present. Here was the opportunity for self-sacrifice of which Mrs. Buxton had spoken to her in her childish days—the time which comes to all, but comes unheeded and unseen to those whose eyes are not trained to watching.

"Mother! could you do without me for a time? If you could, and it would make you easier, and help Edward to—" The word on her lips died away; for it seemed to imply a reproach on one who stood in his shame among them all.

"You would go!" said Mrs. Browne, catching at the unfinished sentence. "Oh! Maggie, that's the best thing you've ever said or done since you were born. Edward, would not you like to have Maggie with you?"

"Yes," said he, "well enough. It would be far better for me than going all alone; though I dare say I could make my way pretty well after a time. If she went, she might stay till I felt settled, and had made some friends, and then she could come back."

Mr. Buxton was astonished at first by this proposal of Maggie's. He could not all at once understand the difference between what she now offered to do, and what he had urged upon her only this very morning. But as he thought about it, he perceived that what was her own she was willing to sacrifice; but that Frank's heart, once given into her faithful keeping, she was answerable for it to him and to God. This light came down upon him slowly; but when he understood, he admired with almost a wondering admiration. That little timid girl brave enough to cross the ocean and go to a foreign land, if she could only help to save her brother!

"I'm sure Maggie," said he, turning towards her, "you are a good, thoughtful little creature. It may be the saving of Edward—I believe it will. I think God will bless you for being so devoted."

"The expense will be doubled," said Edward.

"My dear boy! never mind the money. I can get it advanced upon this cottage."

"As for that, I'll advance it," said Mr. Buxton.

"Could we not," said Maggie, hesitating from her want of knowledge, "make over the furniture—papa's books, and what little plate we have, to Mr. Buxton—something like pawning them—if he would advance the requisite money? He, strange as it may seem, is the only person you can ask in this great strait."

And so it was arranged, after some demur on Mr. Buxton's part. But Maggie kept steadily to her point as soon as she found that it was attainable; and Mrs. Browne was equally inflexible, though from a different feeling. She regarded Mr. Buxton as the cause of her son's banishment, and refused to accept of any favor from him. If there had been time, indeed, she would have preferred obtaining the money in the same manner from any one else. Edward brightened up a little when he heard the sum could be procured; he was almost indifferent how; and, strangely callous, as Maggie thought, he even proposed to draw up a legal form of assignment. Mr. Buxton only thought of hurrying on the departure; but he could not refrain from expressing his approval and admiration of Maggie whenever he came near her. Before he went, he called her aside.

"My dear, I'm not sure if Frank can do better than marry you, after all. Mind! I've not given it as much thought as I should like. But if you come back as we plan, next autumn, and he is steady to you till then—and Edward is going on well—(if he can but keep good, he'll do, for he is very sharp—yon is a knowing paper he drew up)—why, I'll think about it. Only let Frank see a bit of the world first. I'd rather you did not tell him I've any thoughts of coming round, that he may have a fair trial; and I'll keep it from Erminia if I can, or she will let it all out to him. I shall see you to-morrow at the coach. God bless you, my girl, and keep you on the great wide sea." He was absolutely in tears when he went away—tears of admiring regret over Maggie.

Chapter X.

The more Maggie thought, the more she felt sure that the impulse on which she had acted in proposing to go with her brother was right. She feared there was little hope for his character, whatever there might be for his worldly fortune, if he were thrown, in the condition of mind in which he was now, among the set of adventurous men who are continually going over to America in search of an El Dorado to be discovered by their wits. She knew she had but little influence over him at present; but she would not doubt or waver in her hope that patience and love might work him right at last. She meant to get some employment—in teaching—in needlework—in a shop—no matter how humble—and be no burden to him, and make him a happy home, from which he should feel no wish to wander. Her chief anxiety was about her mother. She did not dwell more than she could help on her long absence from Frank; it was too sad, and yet too necessary. She meant to write and tell him all about herself and Edward. The only thing which she would keep for some happy future should be the possible revelation of the proposal which Mr. Buxton had made, that she should give up her engagement as a condition of his not prosecuting Edward.

There was much sorrowful bustle in the moorland cottage that day. Erminia brought up a portion of the money Mr. Buxton was to advance, with an entreaty that Edward would not show himself out of his home; and an account of a letter from Mr. Henry, stating that the Woodchester police believed him to be in London, and that search was being made for him there.

Erminia looked very grave and pale. She gave her message to Mrs. Browne, speaking little beyond what was absolutely necessary. Then she took Maggie aside, and suddenly burst into tears.

"Maggie, darling—what is this going to America? You've always and always been sacrificing yourself to your family, and now you're setting off, nobody knows where, in some vain hope of reforming Edward. I wish he was not your brother, that I might speak of him as I should like."

"He has been doing what is very wrong," said Maggie. "But you—none of you—know his good points—nor how he has been exposed to all sorts of bad influences, I am sure; and never had the advantage of a father's training and friendship, which are so inestimable to a son. O, Minnie! when I remember how we two used to kneel down in the evenings at my father's knee, and say our prayers; and then listen in awe-struck silence to his earnest blessing, which grew more like a prayer for us as his life waned away, I would do anything for Edward rather than that wrestling agony of supplication should have been in vain. I think of him as the little innocent boy, whose arm was round me as if to support me in the Awful Presence, whose true name of Love we had not learned. Minnie! he has had no proper training—no training, I mean, to enable him to resist temptation—and he has been thrown into it without warning or advice. Now he knows what it is; and I must try, though I am but an unknowing girl, to warn and to strengthen him. Don't weaken my faith. Who can do right if we lose faith in them?"

"And Frank!" said Erminia, after a pause. "Poor Frank!"

"Dear Frank!" replied Maggie, looking up, and trying to smile; but, in spite of herself, her eyes filled with tears. "If I could have asked him, I know he would approve of what I am going to do. He would feel it to be right that I should make every effort—I don't mean," said she, as the tears would fall down her cheeks in spite of her quivering effort at a smile, "that I should not have liked to have seen him. But it is no use talking of what one would have liked. I am writing a long letter to him at every pause of leisure."

"And I'm keeping you all this time," said Erminia, getting up, yet loath to go. "When do you intend to come back? Let us feel there is a fixed time. America! Why, it's thousands of miles away. Oh, Maggie! Maggie!"

"I shall come back the next autumn, I trust," said Maggie, comforting her friend with many a soft caress. "Edward will be settled then, I hope. You were longer in France, Minnie. Frank was longer away that time he wintered in Italy with Mr. Monro."

Erminia went slowly to the door. Then she turned, right facing Maggie.

"Maggie! tell the truth. Has my uncle been urging you to go? Because if he has, don't trust him; it is only to break off your engagement."

"No, he has not, indeed. It was my own thought at first. Then in a moment I saw the relief it was to my mother—my poor mother! Erminia, the thought of her grief at Edward's absence is the trial; for my sake, you will come often and often, and comfort her in every way you can."

"Yes! that I will; tell me everything I can do for you."
Kissing each other, with long lingering delay they parted.

Nancy would be informed of the cause of the commotion
in the house; and when she had in some degree ascertained its
nature, she wasted no time in asking further questions, but
quietly got up and dressed herself; and appeared among them,
weak and trembling, indeed, but so calm and thoughtful, that her
presence was an infinite help to Maggie.

When day closed in, Edward stole down to the house
once more. He was haggard enough to have been in anxiety and
concealment for a month. But when his body was refreshed, his
spirits rose in a way inconceivable to Maggie. The Spaniards
who went out with Pizarro were not lured on by more fantastic
notions of the wealth to be acquired in the New World than he
was. He dwelt on these visions in so brisk and vivid a manner,
that he even made his mother cease her weary weeping (which
had lasted the livelong day, despite all Maggie's efforts) to look
up and listen to him.

"I'll answer for it," said he: "before long I'll be an
American judge with miles of cotton plantations."

"But in America," sighed out his mother.

"Never mind, mother!" said he, with a tenderness which
made Maggie's heart glad. "If you won't come over to America
to me, why, I'll sell them all, and come back to live in England.
People will forget the scrapes that the rich American got into in
his youth."

"You can pay back Mr. Buxton then," said his mother.

"Oh, yes—of course," replied he, as if falling into a new
and trivial idea.

Thus the evening whiled away. The mother and son sat,
hand in hand, before the little glinting blazing parlor fire, with
the unlighted candles on the table behind. Maggie, busy in

preparations, passed softly in and out. And when all was done that could be done before going to Liverpool, where she hoped to have two days to prepare their outfit more completely, she stole back to her mother's side. But her thoughts would wander off to Frank, "working his way south through all the hunting-counties," as he had written her word. If she had not urged his absence, he would have been here for her to see his noble face once more; but then, perhaps, she might never have had the strength to go.

Late, late in the night they separated. Maggie could not rest, and stole into her mother's room. Mrs. Browne had cried herself to sleep, like a child. Maggie stood and looked at her face, and then knelt down by the bed and prayed. When she arose, she saw that her mother was awake, and had been looking at her.

"Maggie dear! you're a good girl, and I think God will hear your prayer whatever it was for. I cannot tell you what a relief it is to me to think you're going with him. It would have broken my heart else. If I've sometimes not been as kind as I might have been, I ask your forgiveness, now, my dear; and I bless you and thank you for going out with him; for I'm sure he's not well and strong, and will need somebody to take care of him. And you shan't lose with Mr. Frank, for as sure as I see him I'll tell him what a good daughter and sister you've been; and I shall say, for all he is so rich, I think he may look long before he finds a wife for him like our Maggie. I do wish Ned had got that new greatcoat, he says he left behind him at Woodchester." Her mind reverted to her darling son; but Maggie took her short slumber by her mother's side, with her mother's arms around her; and awoke and felt that her sleep had been blessed. At the coach-office the next morning they met Mr. Buxton all ready as if for a journey, but glancing about him as if in fear of some coming enemy.

"I'm going with you to Liverpool," said he. "Don't make any ado about it, please. I shall like to see you off; and I may be of some use to you, and Erminia begged it of me; and, besides, it will keep me out of Mr. Henry's way for a little time, and I'm afraid he will find it all out, and think me very weak; but you see he made me too hard upon Crayston, so I may take it out in a little soft-heartedness toward the son of an old friend."

Just at this moment Erminia came running through the white morning mist all glowing with haste.

"Maggie," said she, "I'm come to take care of your mother. My uncle says she and Nancy must come to us for a long, long visit. Or if she would rather go home, I'll go with her till she feels able to come to us, and do anything I can think of for her. I will try to be a daughter till you come back, Maggie; only don't be long, or Frank and I shall break our hearts."

Maggie waited till her mother had ended her long clasping embrace of Edward, who was subdued enough this morning; and then, with something like Esau's craving for a blessing, she came to bid her mother good-bye, and received the warm caress she had longed for for years. In another moment the coach was away; and before half an hour had elapsed, Combehurst church-spire had been lost in a turn of the road.

Edward and Mr. Buxton did not speak to each other, and Maggie was nearly silent. They reached Liverpool in the afternoon; and Mr. Buxton, who had been there once or twice before, took them directly to some quiet hotel. He was far more anxious that Edward should not expose himself to any chance of recognition than Edward himself. He went down to the Docks to secure berths in the vessel about to sail the next day, and on his return he took Maggie out to make the requisite purchases.

"Did you pay for us, sir?" said Maggie, anxious to ascertain the amount of money she had left, after defraying the passage.

"Yes," replied he, rather confused. "Erminia begged me not to tell you about it, but I can't manage a secret well. You see she did not like the idea of your going as steerage-passengers as you meant to do; and she desired me to take you cabin places for her. It is no doing of mine, my dear. I did not think of it; but now I have seen how crowded the steerage is, I am very glad Erminia had so much thought. Edward might have roughed it well enough there, but it would never have done for you."

"It was very kind of Erminia," said Maggie, touched at this consideration of her friend; "but..."

"Now don't 'but' about it," interrupted he. "Erminia is very rich, and has more money than she knows what to do with. I'm only vexed I did not think of if myself. For Maggie, though I may have my own ways of thinking on some points, I can't be blind to your goodness."

All evening Mr. Buxton was busy, and busy on their behalf. Even Edward, when he saw the attention that was being paid to his physical comfort, felt a kind of penitence; and after choking once or twice in the attempt, conquered his pride (such I call it for want of a better word) so far as to express some regret for his past conduct, and some gratitude for Mr. Buxton's present kindness. He did it awkwardly enough, but it pleased Mr. Buxton.

"Well—well—that's all very right," said he, reddening from his own uncomfortableness of feeling. "Now don't say any more about it, but do your best in America; don't let me feel I've been a fool in letting you off. I know Mr. Henry will think me so. And, above all, take care of Maggie. Mind what she says, and you're sure to go right."

He asked them to go on board early the next day, as he had promised Erminia to see them there, and yet wished to return as soon as he could. It was evident that he hoped, by making his absence as short as possible, to prevent Mr. Henry's ever knowing that he had left home, or in any way connived at Edward's escape.

So, although the vessel was not to sail till the afternoon's tide, they left the hotel soon after breakfast, and went to the "*Anna-Maria.*" They were among the first passengers on board. Mr. Buxton took Maggie down to her cabin. She then saw the reason of his business the evening before. Every store that could be provided was there. A number of books lay on the little table—books just suited to Maggie's taste. "There!" said he, rubbing his hands. "Don't thank me. It's all Erminia's doing. She gave me the list of books. I've not got all; but I think they'll be enough. Just write me one line, Maggie, to say I've done my best."

Maggie wrote with tears in her eyes—tears of love toward the generous Erminia. A few minutes more and Mr. Buxton was gone. Maggie watched him as long as she could see him; and as his portly figure disappeared among the crowd on the pier, her heart sank within her.

Edward's, on the contrary, rose at his absence. The only one, cognizant of his shame and ill-doing, was gone. A new life lay before him, the opening of which was made agreeable to him, by the position in which he found himself placed, as a cabin-passenger; with many comforts provided for him; for although Maggie's wants had been the principal object of Mr. Buxton's attention, Edward was not forgotten.

He was soon among the sailors, talking away in a rather consequential manner. He grew acquainted with the remainder of the cabin-passengers, at least those who arrived before the final bustle began; and kept bringing his sister such little pieces of news as he could collect.

"Maggie, they say we are likely to have a good start, and a fine moonlight night." Away again he went.

"I say, Maggie, that's an uncommonly pretty girl come on board, with those old people in black. Gone down into the cabin, now; I wish you would scrape up an acquaintance with her, and give me a chance."

Chapter XI.

Maggie sat on deck, wrapped in her duffel-cloak; the old familiar cloak, which had been her wrap in many a happy walk in the haunts near her moorland home. The weather was not cold for the time of year, but still it was chilly to any one that was stationary. But she wanted to look her last on the shoals of English people, who crowded backward and forward, like ants, on the pier. Happy people! who might stay among their loved ones. The mocking demons gathered round her, as they gather round all who sacrifice self, tempting. A crowd of suggestive doubts pressed upon her. "Was it really necessary that she should go with Edward? Could she do him any real good? Would he be in any way influenced by her?" Then the demon tried another description of doubt. "Had it ever been her duty to go? She was leaving her mother alone. She was giving Frank much present sorrow. It was not even yet too late!" She could not endure longer; and replied to her own tempting heart.

"I was right to hope for Edward; I am right to give him the chance of steadiness which my presence will give. I am doing what my mother earnestly wished me to do; and what to the last she felt relieved by my doing. I know Frank will feel sorrow, because I myself have such an aching heart; but if I had asked him whether I was not right in going, he would have been too truthful not to have said yes. I have tried to do right, and though I may fail, and evil may seem to arise rather than good out of my endeavor, yet still I will submit to my failure, and try and say 'God's will be done!' If only I might have seen Frank once more, and told him all face to face!"

To do away with such thoughts, she determined no longer to sit gazing, and tempted by the shore; and, giving one look to the land which contained her lover, she went down below, and busied herself, even through her blinding tears, in trying to arrange her own cabin, and Edward's. She heard boat after boat arrive loaded with passengers. She learnt from Edward, who came down to tell her the fact, that there were upwards of two hundred steerage passengers. She felt the tremulous shake which announced that the ship was loosed from her moorings, and being tugged down the river. She wrapped herself up once more, and came on deck, and sat down among the many who were looking their last look at England. The early winter evening was darkening in, and shutting out the Welsh coast, the hills of which were like the hills of home. She was thankful when she became too ill to think and remember.

Exhausted and still, she did not know whether she was sleeping or waking; or whether she had slept since she had thrown herself down on her cot, when suddenly, there was a great rush, and then Edward stood like lightning by her, pulling her up by the arm.

"The ship is on fire—to the deck, Maggie! Fire! Fire!" he shouted, like a maniac, while he dragged her up the stairs—as if the cry of Fire could summon human aid on the great deep. And the cry was echoed up to heaven by all that crowd in an accent of despair.

They stood huddled together, dressed and undressed; now in red lurid light, showing ghastly faces of terror—now in white wreaths of smoke—as far away from the steerage as they could press; for there, up from the hold, rose columns of smoke, and now and then a fierce blaze leaped out, exulting—higher and higher every time; while from each crevice on that part of the deck issued harbingers of the terrible destruction that awaited them.

The sailors were lowering the boats; and above them stood the captain, as calm as if he were on his own hearth at home—his home where he never more should be. His voice was low—was lower; but as clear as a bell in its distinctness; as wise in its directions as collected thought could make it. Some of the steerage passengers were helping; but more were dumb and motionless with affright. In that dead silence was heard a low wail of sorrow, as of numbers whose power was crushed out of them by that awful terror. Edward still held his clutch of Margaret's arm.

"Be ready!" said he, in a fierce whisper.

The fire sprung up along the main-mast, and did not sink or disappear again. They knew then that all the mad efforts made by some few below to extinguish it were in vain; and then went up the prayers of hundreds, in mortal agony of fear:

"Lord! have mercy upon us!"

Not in quiet calm of village church did ever such a pitiful cry go up to heaven; it was like one voice—like the day of judgment in the presence of the Lord.

And after that there was no more silence; but a confusion of terrible farewells, and wild cries of affright, and purposeless rushes hither and thither.

The boats were down, rocking on the sea. The captain spoke:

"Put the children in first; they are the most helpless."

One or two stout sailors stood in the boats to receive them. Edward drew nearer and nearer to the gangway, pulling Maggie with him. She was almost pressed to death, and stifled. Close in her ear, she heard a woman praying to herself. She, poor creature, knew of no presence but God's in that awful hour, and spoke in a low voice to Him.

"My heart's darlings are taken away from me. Faith! faith! Oh, my great God! I will die in peace, if Thou wilt but grant me faith in this terrible hour, to feel that Thou wilt take care of my poor orphans. Hush! dearest Billy," she cried out shrill to a little fellow in the boat waiting for his mother; and the change in her voice from despair to a kind of cheerfulness, showed what a mother's love can do. "Mother will come soon. Hide his face, Anne, and wrap your shawl tight round him." And then her voice sank down again in the same low, wild prayer for faith. Maggie could not turn to see her face, but took the hand which hung near her. The woman clutched at it with the grasp of a vice; but went on praying, as if unconscious. Just then the crowd gave way a little. The captain had said, that the women were to go next; but they were too frenzied to obey his directions, and now pressed backward and forward. The sailors, with mute, stern obedience, strove to follow out the captain's directions. Edward pulled Maggie, and she kept her hold on the mother. The mate, at the head of the gangway, pushed him back.

"Only women are to go!"

"There are men there."

"Three, to manage the boat."

"Come on, Maggie! while there's room for us," said he, unheeding. But Maggie drew back, and put the mother's hand into the mate's. "Save her first!" said she. The woman did not know of anything, but that her children were there; it was only in after days, and quiet hours, that she remembered the young creature who pushed her forward to join her fatherless children, and, by losing her place in the crowd, was jostled—where, she did not know—but dreamed until her dying day. Edward pressed on, unaware that Maggie was not close behind him. He was deaf to reproaches; and, heedless of the hand stretched out to hold him back, sprang toward the boat. The men there pushed her off—full and more than full as she was; and overboard he fell into the sullen heaving waters.

His last shout had been on Maggie's name—a name she never thought to hear again on earth, as she was pressed back, sick and suffocating. But suddenly a voice rang out above all confused voices and moaning hungry waves, and above the roaring fire.

"Maggie, Maggie! My Maggie!"

Out of the steerage side of the crowd a tall figure issued forth, begrimed with smoke. She could not see, but she knew. As a tame bird flutters to the human breast of its protector when affrighted by some mortal foe, so Maggie fluttered and cowered into his arms. And, for a moment, there was no more terror or thought of danger in the hearts of those twain, but only infinite and absolute peace. She had no wonder how he came there: it was enough that he was there. He first thought of the destruction that was present with them. He was as calm and composed as if they sat beneath the thorn-tree on the still moorlands, far away. He took her, without a word, to the end of the quarter-deck. He lashed her to a piece of spar. She never spoke:

"Maggie," he said, "my only chance is to throw you overboard. This spar will keep you floating. At first, you will go down—deep, deep down. Keep your mouth and eyes shut. I shall be there when you come up. By God's help, I will struggle bravely for you."

She looked up; and by the flashing light he could see a trusting, loving smile upon her face. And he smiled back at her; a grave, beautiful look, fit to wear on his face in heaven. He helped her to the side of the vessel, away from the falling burning pieces of mast. Then for a moment he paused.

"If—Maggie, I may be throwing you in to death." He put his hand before his eyes. The strong man lost courage. Then she spoke:

"I am not afraid; God is with us, whether we live or die!" She looked as quiet and happy as a child on its mother's breast! and so before he lost heart again, he heaved her up, and threw her as far as he could over into the glaring, dizzying water; and straight leaped after her. She came up with an involuntary look of terror on her face; but when she saw him by the red glare of the burning ship, close by her side, she shut her eyes, and looked as if peacefully going to sleep. He swam, guiding the spar.

"I think we are near Llandudno. I know we have passed the little Ormes' head." That was all he said; but she did not speak.

He swam out of the heat and fierce blaze of light into the quiet, dark waters; and then into the moon's path. It might be half an hour before he got into that silver stream. When the beams fell down upon them he looked at Maggie. Her head rested on the spar, quite still. He could not bear it. "Maggie—dear heart! speak!"

With a great effort she was called back from the borders of death by that voice, and opened her filmy eyes, which looked abroad as if she could see nothing nearer than the gleaming lights of Heaven. She let the lids fall softly again. He was as if alone in the wide world with God.

"A quarter of an hour more and all is over," thought he. "The people at Llandudno must see our burning ship, and will come out in their boats." He kept in the line of light, although it did not lead him direct to the shore, in order that they might be seen. He swam with desperation. One moment he thought he had heard her last gasp rattle through the rush of the waters; and all strength was gone, and he lay on the waves as if he himself must die, and go with her spirit straight through that purple lift to heaven; the next he heard the splash of oars, and raised himself and cried aloud. The boatmen took them in—and examined her by the lantern—and spoke in Welsh—and shook their heads. Frank threw himself on his knees, and prayed them to take her to land. They did not know his words, but they understood his prayer. He kissed her lips—he chafed her hands—he wrung the water out of her hair—he held her feet against his warm breast.

"She is not dead," he kept saying to the men, as he saw their sorrowful, pitying looks.

The kind people at Llandudno had made ready their own humble beds, with every appliance of comfort they could think of, as soon as they understood the nature of the calamity which had befallen the ship on their coasts. Frank walked, dripping, bareheaded, by the body of his Margaret, which was borne by some men along the rocky sloping shore.

"She is not dead!" he said. He stopped at the first house they came to. It belonged to a kind-hearted woman. They laid Maggie in her bed, and got the village doctor to come and see her.

"There is life still," said he, gravely.

"I knew it," said Frank. But it felled him to the ground. He sank first in prayer, and then in insensibility. The doctor did everything. All that night long he passed to and fro from house to house; for several had swum to Llandudno. Others, it was thought, had gone to Abergele.

In the morning Frank was recovered enough to write to his father, by Maggie's bedside. He sent the letter off to Conway by a little bright-looking Welsh boy. Late in the afternoon she awoke.

In a moment or two she looked eagerly round her, as if gathering in her breath; and then she covered her head and sobbed.

"Where is Edward?" asked she.

"We do not know," said Frank, gravely. "I have been round the village, and seen every survivor here; he is not among them, but he may be at some other place along the coast."

She was silent, reading in his eyes his fears—his belief.

At last she asked again.

"I cannot understand it. My head is not clear. There are such rushing noises in it. How came you there?" She shuddered involuntarily as she recalled the terrible where.

For an instant he dreaded, for her sake, to recall the circumstances of the night before; but then he understood how her mind would dwell upon them until she was satisfied.

"You remember writing to me, love, telling me all. I got your letter—I don't know how long ago—yesterday, I think. Yes! in the evening. You could not think, Maggie, I would let you go alone to America. I won't speak against Edward, poor fellow! but we must both allow that he was not the person to watch over you as such a treasure should be watched over. I thought I would go with you. I hardly know if I meant to make myself known to you all at once, for I had no wish to have much to do with your brother. I see now that it was selfish in me. Well! there was nothing to be done, after receiving your letter, but to set off for Liverpool straight, and join you. And after that

decision was made, my spirits rose, for the old talks about
Canada and Australia came to my mind, and this seemed like a
realization of them. Besides, Maggie, I suspected—I even
suspect now—that my father had something to do with your
going with Edward?"

"Indeed, Frank!" said she, earnestly, "you are mistaken; I
cannot tell you all now; but he was so good and kind at last. He
never urged me to go; though, I believe, he did tell me it would
be the saving of Edward."

"Don't agitate yourself, love. I trust there will be time
enough, some happy day at home, to tell me all. And till then, I
will believe that my father did not in any way suggest this
voyage. But you'll allow that, after all that has passed, it was not
unnatural in me to suppose so. I only told Middleton I was
obliged to leave him by the next train. It was not till I was fairly
off, that I began to reckon up what money I had with me. I doubt
even if I was sorry to find it was so little. I should have to put
forth my energies and fight my way, as I had often wanted to do.
I remember, I thought how happy you and I would be, striving
together as poor people 'in that new world which is the old.'
Then you had told me you were going in the steerage; and that
was all suitable to my desires for myself."

"It was Erminia's kindness that prevented our going
there. She asked your father to take us cabin places unknown to
me."

"Did she? dear Erminia! it is just like her. I could almost
laugh to remember the eagerness with which I doffed my signs
of wealth, and put on those of poverty. I sold my watch when I
got into Liverpool—yesterday, I believe—but it seems like
months ago. And I rigged myself out at a slop-shop with suitable
clothes for a steerage passenger. Maggie! you never told me the
name of the vessel you were going to sail in!"

"I did not know it till I got to Liverpool. All Mr. Buxton said was, that some ship sailed on the 15th."

"I concluded it must be the *Anna-Maria,* (poor *Anna-Maria!*) and I had no time to lose. She had just heaved her anchor when I came on board. Don't you recollect a boat hailing her at the last moment? There were three of us in her."

"No! I was below in my cabin—trying not to think," said she, coloring a little.

"Well! as soon as I got on board it began to grow dark, or, perhaps, it was the fog on the river; at any rate, instead of being able to single out your figure at once, Maggie—it is one among a thousand—I had to go peering into every woman's face; and many were below. I went between decks, and by-and-by I was afraid I had mistaken the vessel; I sat down—I had no spirit to stand; and every time the door opened I roused up and looked—but you never came. I was thinking what to do; whether to be put on shore in Ireland, or to go on to New York, and wait for you there;—if was the worst time of all, for I had nothing to do; and the suspense was horrible. I might have known," said he, smiling, "my little Emperor of Russia was not one to be a steerage passenger."

But Maggie was too much shaken to smile; and the thought of Edward lay heavy upon her mind.

"Then the fire broke out; how, or why, I suppose will never be ascertained. It was at our end of the vessel. I thanked God, then, that you were not there. The second mate wanted some one to go down with him to bring up the gunpowder, and throw it overboard. I had nothing to do, and I went. We wrapped it up in wet sails, but it was a ticklish piece of work, and took time. When we had got it overboard, the flames were gathering far and wide. I don't remember what I did until I heard Edward's voice speaking your name."

It was decided that the next morning they should set off homeward, striving on their way to obtain tidings of Edward. Frank would have given his only valuable, (his mother's diamond-guard, which he wore constantly), as a pledge for some advance of money; but the kind Welsh people would not have it. They had not much spare cash, but what they had they readily lent to the survivors of the *Anna-Maria*. Dressed in the homely country garb of the people, Frank and Maggie set off in their car. If was a clear, frosty morning; the first that winter. The road soon lay high up on the cliffs along the coast. They looked down on the sea rocking below. At every village they stopped, and Frank inquired, and made the driver inquire in Welsh; but no tidings gained they of Edward; though here and there Maggie watched Frank into some cottage or other, going to see a dead body, beloved by some one: and when he came out, solemn and grave, their sad eyes met, and she knew it was not he they sought, without needing words.

At Abergele they stopped to rest; and because, being a larger place, it would need a longer search, Maggie lay down on the sofa, for she was very weak, and shut her eyes, and tried not to see forever and ever that mad struggling crowd lighted by the red flames.

Frank came back in an hour or so; and soft behind him— laboriously treading on tiptoe—Mr. Buxton followed. He was evidently choking down his sobs; but when he saw the white wan figure of Maggie, he held out his arms.

"My dear! my daughter!" he said, "God bless you!" He could not speak more—he was fairly crying; but he put her hand in Frank's and kept holding them both.

"My father," said Frank, speaking in a husky voice, while his eyes filled with tears, "had heard of it before he received my letter. I might have known that the lighthouse signals would take it fast to Liverpool. I had written a few lines to him saying I was going to you; happily they never reached—that was spared to my dear father."

Maggie saw the look of restored confidence that passed between father and son.

"My mother?" said she at last.

"She is here," said they both at once, with sad solemnity.

"Oh, where? Why did not you tell me?" exclaimed she, starting up. But their faces told her why.

"Edward is drowned—is dead," said she, reading their looks.

There was no answer.

"Let me go to my mother."

"Maggie, she is with him. His body was washed ashore last night. My father and she heard of it as they came along. Can you bear to see her? She will not leave him."

"Take me to her," Maggie answered.

They led her into a bed-room. Stretched on the bed lay Edward, but now so full of hope and worldly plans.

Mrs. Browne looked round, and saw Maggie. She did not get up from her place by his head; nor did she long avert her gaze from his poor face. But she held Maggie's hand, as the girl knelt by her, and spoke to her in a hushed voice, undisturbed by tears. Her miserable heart could not find that relief.

"He is dead!—he is gone!—he will never come back again! If he had gone to America—it might have been years first—but he would have come back to me. But now he will never come back again;—never—never!"

Her voice died away, as the wailings of the night-wind die in the distance; and there was silence—silence more sad and hopeless than any passionate words of grief.

And to this day it is the same. She prizes her dead son more than a thousand living daughters, happy and prosperous as is Maggie now—rich in the love of many. If Maggie did not show such reverence to her mother's faithful sorrows, others might wonder at her refusal to be comforted by that sweet daughter. But Maggie treats her with such tender sympathy, never thinking of herself or her own claims, that Frank, Erminia, Mr. Buxton, Nancy, and all, are reverent and sympathizing too.

Over both old and young the memory of one who is dead broods like a dove—of one who could do but little during her lifetime—who was doomed only to "stand and wait"—who was meekly content to *be* gentle, holy, patient, and undefiled—the memory of the invalid Mrs. Buxton.

"THERE'S ROSEMARY FOR REMEMBRANCE."

The End

CPSIA information can be obtained at www.ICGtesting.com
Printed in the USA
LVOW050624260612

287677LV00001B/35/A

9 781934 648292